Best Books for Ya

W9-AHO-782

The
Country
of the Heart

Books by Barbara Wersba

The Dream Watcher
Run Softly, Go Fast
The Country of the Heart

The Country of the Heart

BARBARA WERSBA

Atheneum New York

1975

The lines from "Preludes for Memnon" are from
Collected Poems by Conrad Aiken. Copyright © 1953, 1970
by Conrad Aiken. Reprinted by permission
of Oxford University Press, Inc.

Library of Congress Cataloging in Publication Data

Wersba, Barbara.   The country of the heart.
SUMMARY: A young man describes the joys and
anguish of his relationship with a famous woman poet
who comes to his town to live as a recluse.
[1. Poets—Fiction. 2. Love—Fiction] I. Title.
PZ7.W473Co   [Fic]   75-6947

ISBN 0-689-30469-2

The
Country
of the Heart

Hadley, you have been gone for five years—years scattered like dust—and since I never told you how I felt, never once spoke of the depth of my love for you, love made foolish by being young, let me tell it to you now: weaving a song for you out of the wind, striking phrases onto the air like metal, shaping words that you would have liked, because words were the only things you cared for.

Let me tell you how it was in those days.

Let me find you again in the country of the heart.

two

You were walking down a long lane of trees. It was autumn and the maples were gold against a dark sky. Leaves as bright as coins whirled down on you, and yet you didn't see them. It had rained a few hours earlier and everything was intensified: burnished leaves, gunmetal clouds, and walking through these colors, blindly, a woman with no expression on her face. I was waiting for the school bus, and as you

3

came nearer my heart tightened. You were wearing slacks and a tweed jacket, and by your side trotted a homely little dog. Then you passed me, close enough to touch, and within the space of a second I knew that something had changed. I knew that my life had turned a corner and that I would not be allowed to go back. I watched you walk away and all of it seemed to have happened before—your thin figure moving down the lane, the little dog, the bleak morning sky—and I felt afraid.

The bus came and Jerry and I got on—spilling our books onto the nearest seat. I pressed my face against the window, hoping for one more glimpse of you, but the sky went black and it started to rain again. "Hey Steve, you know who that was? The lady with the dog?" Jerry asked. I shook my head. "Hadley Norman. The writer."

I took out a cigarette, but didn't light it. Finally I put it away again. "What's wrong?" Jerry asked.

"Nothing," I said.

"You ever hear of her? Hadley Norman?"

"Yes."

"Is she famous?"

"Yes. Sure."

"It's funny. I never heard of her. But my mother says she's a well-known poet. She's rented the carriage house."

Jerry went on talking, but I didn't hear him. It was as though all sound had been blotted out and nothing in the world existed but the image of your receding figure, walking down a lane of trees. After a few minutes Jerry moved

4

across the aisle to talk to some other kids, and I was left alone. I reached in my back pocket and took out a paperback, worn with use. It was called *Three Landscapes: Poems by Hadley Norman*—and now I was trembling because I realized that I had known who you were by instinct, without ever having seen a picture of you. On my desk at home were all of your books, and in a loose-leaf binder I had pasted reviews of these books and an interview you had done for the *New York Times*. I admired you more than any other American poet, and the fact that our paths had just crossed—in the midst of storm-light, rain, whirling leaves—made my heart sink. I had no joy in seeing you that first time because I knew that it would be impossible to meet you—that fame surrounded you like a wall.

The bus pulled up in front of the Community College and Jerry joined me again. It was pouring by now, so we made a dash for the main entrance. We stood there, soaking wet, and this time I took out the cigarette and lit it. "Listen," I began, trying to sound casual.

"What?" he said.

"That poet. Mrs. Norman. How come she's rented the carriage house?"

"I don't know. My mother says she came up here to finish a book or something. But it's weird. I mean, who would move here voluntarily?"

Silently I agreed with him, because of all the places on earth, Cromwell, New York was the ugliest: a town where the old mansions were going to ruin and no new houses were being built. A Hudson River town that had once had a factory, but the factory had closed, leaving only a main street and a grocery store, and a library that was never open. Frame houses dotted the hillside like toys, but the view of the river was spoiled because pollution drifted up from the city and cast a yellow haze on the water. Barges would pass, pushed by tugboats, and there was always the sound of a train somewhere, rattling its lonely way to Albany. But every autumn I would watch the geese migrate, high and swift like arrows, their voices trailing in the wind, and I would feel a sense of hope—as though the changing seasons could effect a change in me.

Hadley, I could not have known that you had come to this dying town because you yourself were dying—that you wanted bleakness that winter instead of beauty: gray weather, silence, and mist shrouding the river. I could not have known that the one thing you needed was solitude— time in which to understand yourself—and so I broke your solitude like glass. How could I have known anything in those days? I was eighteen. I was asleep. Nothing had ever touched me.

three

We stood on the steps with a curtain of rain beyond us and Jerry said, "I have to go. I'll be late for Spanish."

"OK," I said to him. "See you at lunch."

But instead of going to class, I went to the school library and sat by the window. I saw you walking away from me—down that lane of yellow-spinning leaves—and I felt that time had stopped and that for the rest of my life you would be walking away from me, like someone in a nightmare, walking farther and farther away without moving at all. I had been writing poems since I was twelve years old, but every time I sent one to a magazine it would come back with a letter of rejection—and when I compared myself to someone like you, I felt despair. And there was no one to talk to. Not a single person in my life who understood poetry. But somewhere an ocean glittered, and spires rose out of dust, and faraway birds plunged into the horizon.

All beyond my reach.

I took *Three Landscapes* out of my pocket again and turned to the last poem.

There, in that wakening zone of lament, there, with daggers and horsemen clashing their steel, there, always there, with the taste of the world in my mouth and a terrified heart in the dawn—from that circle of fear I go down to the sea and its light.

Everywhere emptiness, luminous water, a tidal pool throbbing with gold. The dunes drift themselves into magnified angels and rise in the wind. I hear them come singing, their hair blown with sun, and their wings are the arms of the sky.

Half-prose, half-dream. Nine books published plus a volume of *Collected Poems*. Prizes won. Interviews given.

7

Was it those things I wanted, or simply to be a poet? I didn't know. I worshipped writers so much that I sometimes felt it was the title I wanted rather than the profession—yet I worked at my writing every day. I also collected masses of books, and when I could not afford to buy them, stole them from the school library. All of these things swam together in my mind, and by the end of the afternoon I was silent and angry. Jerry and I had a fight going home on the bus, a stupid one, and we parted without speaking. Then I slipped into the house, went up the back stairs and locked myself in my room. I felt like a mad detective, looking for clues when there had been no crime.

In the loose-leaf binder on my desk was an article about you that I had cut out of the newspaper—and it said that you had been born in Boston, educated at Hunter College, and had taught at the New School. It said that you were divorced from a critic named John Norman, had no children, and that you were forty years old. It said that your first book had been published when you were only nineteen.

You had been the prodigy of the New York literary world while still a student, and after graduation had moved in with a group of artists in Brooklyn Heights. All of these people were famous—poets, painters, musicians—and I had sometimes tried to picture your life in that brownstone house where everyone had his own workroom, and slept at odd hours, and stayed up late at night drinking wine and talking. It sounded like paradise to me—and yet imagining it only increased my loneliness.

That evening at dinner my father turned to me and said, "When are you going to rake those leaves?"

I looked up from my food with a blank face. "What?"

"The *leaves,* mister, the leaves. I asked you to rake them ten days ago."

"I'll do it soon."

"What is that supposed to mean?"

"I said I'll do it soon!" I answered. "Leave me alone."

"You raise your voice to me once more and I'll lock you up for a month," he said, rising to his feet.

"I said I'll rake your stupid leaves!"

"Why, you little bastard," he said softly. "I ought to throw you through that window."

My sister was watching closely and the table was very still. Before anything could happen, I pushed back my chair and went outdoors, breathing deeply to control myself. I could smell the smoke from our fireplace and above my head stars raced through a stormy sky. Then the clouds parted and the moon flooded the world—and for a moment I felt dizzy and wild, wanting something and not knowing what it was. All the poetry I had ever read was going through my mind—words so beautiful that they hurt me—and I feared that I would never equal those words, that my life would come to nothing, that I would turn into a person like my father.

So I ran all the way to your house and stood in the cold moonlight watching your door. I was to stand there for many nights before I met you. And I was to conjure you so wrongly that your reality would seem bizarre. I thought you were a goddess, a legend, a myth, a candle blazing in wind.

A face in the sea.

four

Hadley, my father has been in a veterans' hospital for two years, paralyzed from a stroke, and my sister is gone—run away, traveling the continent of America in blue jeans and a poncho and long dark pigtails. My mother who smiled perpetually, whose most frequent words were, "Everything will be fine," no longer smiles, but has grown silent and old. I look back on these people and realize that we shared the same house, the same intimacies, but were strangers. Two children and two adults: afraid to love one another, living our lives in unspoken despair. I see my father sitting angrily in front of the television set, not seeing the program. I see my mother baking pound cakes for the church bazaar. I see them—like figures in a painting—sitting round the dinner table, the conversation perfunctory and dull, my sister and I glancing at each other occasionally with a shared secret. Sally was the only one I related to— because she was a rebel, I guess, and the life in her would not be killed.

I understand my father's anger now and even sense that

it was justified. This grossly masculine man, who had served so eagerly in the Korean War, whose sole need was for adventure, wound up running a small business and supporting a family. Wound up sacrificing everything for his children. And his disappointment in us was so great that once, in the middle of a fight with me, he started to cry—frustration sending tears down his face—his memories of freedom and adventure torturing him with all the might-have-beens of his life. It fills me with sadness that I made a point of provoking him in those days, that I would go out of my way to annoy him. He hated my poetry, my books, my moodiness, and was always asking me why I couldn't be like other kids. "What is it with you?" he yelled at me once. "Do you *want* to be a freak?"

I can still smell the fragrance of my mother's kitchen and see little plants on the windowsill. I can still see her going off to church and coming home to cook the Sunday meal. I see all of her small-town ways—she who was a minister's daughter—and realize that she believed in those ways and in the concept of family. She spoke of her mother's people in fond and dreamy tones, as though they were characters in a novel, and was always mentioning some relative unknown to us: a distant uncle, a cousin who had died tragically, an eccentric aunt. She told endless tales of her great-grandmother who had staked out a claim on the Kansas prairie by simply living on it, alone in a hut, throughout a deep and snowblind winter. I hear her voice telling these stories and feel yesterday inside me.

I wonder what you would have thought had you seen me standing in front of your house, Hadley—staring at the windows and humming to myself, trying to keep warm. I froze during those November evenings, fearing to move lest my feet crackle the leaves, darting behind a tree whenever you passed the window, watching with intensity as a light went on or off. The simple act of standing there helped me—your presence in the world making me feel that I might survive. And the fact that we both lived at the same point in history was almost mystical to me. I did not know you and yet you were *there,* moving through time and space in the same way I was, waking to the same pale sunlight, watching the same skies flow toward winter.

I began to look for you in the mornings, thinking that you walked your dog every day at the same time, but never saw you. I asked Information for your phone number, only to learn that it was unlisted. You had chosen to live in the one isolated house in our neighborhood—a stone barn on the grounds of an estate—and surrounding you were four acres of woods. The building had been a carriage house once, was inadequately heated, and always for rent. And because I believed that all writers were rich, I could not understand why you had selected such a place.

I lay in bed at night and tried to picture you, but your existence loomed so much larger than life that it was impossible to see you doing ordinary things—shopping for groceries or cleaning house. I wondered if you had a maid, and if your world was crowded with events: literary parties, famous friends, trips to Europe. I thought of the rooms you probably lived in in New York—opulent and booklined. I imagined skylights, fresh flowers, a scent of perfume.

I read your books again and found an article you had written for the *Saturday Review*. Then I began to memorize your poems, as if knowing them by heart would make you more accessible. After that I wrote you a fan letter and tore it up. I even asked the boy at the post office if your mail was delivered or whether you collected it yourself. He wasn't sure. And so, when all possibilities had been exhausted and there was no place left to turn—when I had gone over the thing in my mind a hundred times, when I felt almost sick from the knowledge that you would leave Cromwell one day and move back to the city—only then did I find the courage to walk up to your house and knock on the door. It was Saturday, ten A.M., and I was terrified.

five

No one answered the door, so I pulled on the antique ship's bell over my head and it made a loud clang. In my pocket were several of my poems, neatly typed, and under my arm was a new copy of *Three Landscapes*. I had slicked down my curly hair and was wearing a tie for the first time in months. For a second my mind flashed back to the day when I had discovered you—standing in the library flipping through an anthology of modern poems—and I remembered the chill that had gone down my back when I read your words.

Moments passed. I heard you coming down the stairs and the door was flung open. The speech I had prepared sank out of my mind.

You were not the same woman I had seen on the road. The same person, yes, but different in looks: smaller somehow, and unkempt. You were wearing a faded plaid bathrobe, and slippers, and horn-rimmed glasses. A cigarette burned between your fingers. Your short blond hair was messy, as though you had been running your hands through it, and I saw at once that this hair was streaked with gray. I saw that your mouth was thin and angry, and that you were not beautiful.

"What is it?" you said.

"Mrs. Norman . . ." I began. "Mrs. Norman, excuse me for barging in this way, but I'm a neighbor, and a fan of yours, and since your phone is unlisted I couldn't call you. So I . . . I just came over wondering if you would autograph this book. I mean, I would consider it a great favor."

You looked at me with the longest, coldest look I had ever seen. "Did it ever occur to you that my phone is unlisted for a reason?"

"I beg your pardon?"

"Writers *write* in the morning. Or didn't you know that?"

"No, I didn't. I mean . . ."

14

An expression of wild impatience came over your face. "Oh, for Christ's sake, give me your pen. I'll sign the book."

I felt myself going scarlet. "I didn't bring a pen."

You sighed. Paused. Then came to a decision. "All right —come upstairs."

I followed you up the wooden stairway like someone going to an execution—noticing, despite my panic, that the first floor of the house was an old stable. The second floor was even more surprising: a cavernous room with a huge stone fireplace, high beamed ceiling, and shabby furniture. The card table you had been working at was near the window, and around a corner I could see a small kitchen which was in a state of chaos. Everywhere I looked there were empty glasses and magazines and cigarette butts. Your dog was asleep on a chair.

You sat down at the card table, pushed some papers aside, and I handed you the book.

"What's your name?" you asked.

"Steven Harper."

You scrawled something in the book and gave it back to me. "All right. There's your autograph."

But I couldn't let it go at that. The scene was being played wrong. Everything I had planned was collapsing. I stared at you and saw an irritable face and guarded blue eyes—and I could not connect this face with the poems you wrote.

"Mrs. Norman . . ."

"Well?"

"If I had known you were working, I wouldn't have barged in this way. But I didn't. So I hope you'll accept my apology."

You gazed at me. "I accept it."

"I mean, I'm a great fan of yours. I've been reading your stuff for years."

"Really?"

"Yes. I admire your style tremendously."

"In what sense?"

I groped for the right words. "In the sense that it's so . . . original."

You rose to your feet. "And the rest of the story goes like this: you want to be a poet, but aren't sure you have talent. And you would like me to read your work, but are afraid to ask. And you hope that because we are neighbors, you can insinuate yourself into my life."

I felt as if you had struck me.

"Well, I want you to understand something. I never read the work of students. And your 'barging in,' as you so delicately put it, is a great imposition on me."

"I'm sorry," I stammered.

But you had already gone into the kitchen and were plugging in an electric coffeepot. I stood there, numb with misery, and felt the seconds pass. Your dog woke up and stretched. A log in the fireplace burst into a shower of sparks.

At the far end of the room a staircase led to an open loft —the bedroom—and I could see the surface of an unmade bed. Clothes were strewn about, and there were books and newspapers on the floor. I glanced at the card table and saw that you had been writing poetry on a yellow legal pad. The wastebasket was full of crumpled yellow sheets.

You came back into the room, a coffee mug in your hand. "Still here?" you asked coldly.

I tried to reply, but no words came.

"Well, you'll have to go. I want to get back to work."

Unable to say good-bye, to speak or even look at you, I turned on my heel and went down the stairs. Carefully, I closed the front door and walked along the narrow country lane. And when I could no longer see the house, and the woods surrounded me, when I could no longer control the way I felt or steel myself against the enormity of my disappointment, I leaned against a tree and wept.

six

The flicker of leaves. The quiet sound of leaves falling. A dappled grove—sunlight spilling through branches. Squirrels. Birds plundering berries. Red and gold, and the dry sound of leaves drifting, spinning, covering my feet. The world sleeps under the leaves and insects burrow—waiting for winter. On the gray river a tugboat hoots its horn. The morning train rattles its way to Albany. And the grove is so still, so breathless and silent, that I can hear the thundering of my heart.

17

seven

For the next three weeks I wrote like someone possessed, trying to put you out of my mind by sheer labor, writing poems in notebooks and on the back of envelopes, rushing home from school each day to hide in my room and work. I cut classes and sat in the college library writing poems. And when I was not writing them, I was reading them: Rilke, Pound, Joyce, Eliot, Yeats. The one poet I omitted was Hadley Norman, because your books were now stacked in my closet. I knew this was childish, but you had hurt me so badly that the pain was almost physical. The only way to find wholeness again was work.

My twelve-year-old sister fought with my father. My father locked her in her room. My mother baked endlessly for the church cake sale, giving our house the atmosphere of an armed camp stuffed with cookies. The trees were bare and winter sunsets were beginning—the sky swept with slate and amber, and crows drifting over the fields. The nights became crisp, stars flung across the firmament like diamonds, and I tossed and turned in my sleep. I dreamed that I went to the carriage house and that you walked out of the door dressed in white, your arms stretched toward me. I dreamed that it was summer and we sat together by a lake, huge butterflies trembling in the air. I dreamed—crazily—that you married my father and bore him a child.

I wrote in my journal, took long walks at twilight, helped my sister with her homework. I made a halfhearted attempt to date a girl named Marjorie Turner—but she refused. Jerry and I hung around Wilson's in the evenings, the local beer joint, but I soon found that I had no capacity for drinking. It made me sick. And all the while I knew that I was simply filling time, treading water, waiting for something to happen.

One evening at dusk I took a walk down Highgate Road, near your house. It was very cold and I had my hands thrust in the pockets of my jacket. A little dog passed me, trotting fast, and it had disappeared before I realized that it was your dog. I turned and saw it in the distance, heading for the intersection—and then I began to run. I had never run so fast in my life, trees whizzing by me, my breath coming in sobs, and just before the dog reached the traffic light, I grabbed him. To my surprise he didn't protest, but started to lick my face.

I stood there holding him, and it must have been a full two minutes before I realized that I would have to bring him home.

eight

All the lights were on in your house, and for a moment it looked like a stage setting: a castle placed against a purple sky. You were standing in the driveway with a flashlight, wearing the same plaid bathrobe I had seen you in before, and as you heard the sound of my feet on gravel, you shot the beam of light toward me.

"Mrs. Norman?" I said. "It's Steven Harper. I found your dog."

You ran up to me and I saw that your eyes were frantic. "Where was he?"

"On Highgate Road. He was running toward the intersection."

"My God."

"I caught him just in time. Did he get loose by accident?"

You took the dog from me and buried your face in his wiry hair. For a long while you simply held him, and I realized—with a dim sense of shock—that he was the most important thing in your life.

"What's his name?" I ventured carefully.

"Sam."

"He's nice looking."

You gave me an irritable glance. "No, he's not. But we're very close."

"Is he some kind of terrier?"

"No. Just a mutt."

Silence came over us and we stood in the twilight without speaking. I could see you shivering in the bathrobe, and I knew that you were fighting a small battle between asking me to come indoors and dismissing me. I could feel—almost palpably—how much you wanted to be alone, and yet I couldn't bring myself to leave.

Finally you said, "Well, would you like to come indoors? It's freezing out here."

I felt my heart pounding. "OK. Thank you."

We went up the staircase, Sam still in your arms, and when we reached the top I saw that the living room was even messier than it had been the last time. "Sit down," you said. "I want to give Sam his dinner."

Left alone, I gazed around the huge room. A fire was crackling and there was a blanket on the worn couch. To one side of the couch was a table with books on it, a bottle of English gin, and a half-empty glass. There were piles of magazines on the floor, and rubber dog toys.

You came out of the kitchen with a glass in your hand. "Do you want a drink?"

"All right," I said. "Thank you."

You sat next to me on the couch and reached for the liquor bottle. Then you poured each of us a full tumbler of gin, gave me mine, and moved away to sit on a chair. I made a pretense of sipping my drink—hating the taste of it.

I looked at you and saw that you were staring into the fire. And suddenly your thinness, the plaid bathrobe, and your untidy hair struck at my heart. Without knowing why, I felt pity for you.

You glanced at me. "Where did you say you lived?"

"Just down the road. Cromwell Lane."

"I see. And you go to college, I suppose?"

"The Community College. But it isn't very good."

"Why not?"

"Because . . . well, there aren't any good English courses."

"Ah, I'd forgotten. You're a budding poet."

"I never said that, Mrs. Norman."

"You don't need to. *Poet* is written across your face in capital letters. May I give you some advice?"

I looked up quickly. "Yes. Sure."

"Forget the whole thing. It's a lousy profession."

I couldn't reply to that one, so silence descended on us again. Sam trotted into the room and you took him on your lap, murmuring something I couldn't hear. He growled playfully and you ruffled his ears. I felt drawn to you as though there were a magnet between us—as though a cord were pulling me into your life—yet at the same time there was a reticence, a strange aversion.

You finished the glass of gin and asked me to refill it. I did so, and sat down. The silence in the room was terrible, baffling, and after a while I could hear a clock ticking somewhere, its small voice insistent and remote.

"Why do you want to be a poet?" you asked.

"I . . . I don't know," I said. "I just do."

"How old are you?"

"Eighteen."

"I see. Well, you'll get over it."

A wave of anger passed through me. "I don't think so, Mrs. Norman. I've been writing for years. Writing is all I care about."

You put Sam gently on the floor and went to stand by the fireplace. Your eyes were thoughtful, veiled, and I realized that you hadn't been listening to me. Then you finished the second glass of gin and I saw that you were beginning to get drunk.

"I wouldn't be eighteen again for gold. Nor would I have chosen to be a writer. But you don't choose."

"How do you mean?"

"You don't choose writing—it chooses you. And then it drives you and drives you until you're burned out, and there's nothing to show for it. Don't you understand? People don't need poetry. It isn't good for anything."

"But you're a great poet," I said softly.

You whirled on me. "Be quiet! You don't even know what you're talking about. The only thing that matters in life is connecting. Connecting with another human being. Or maybe with God. But this form of play we call art is meaningless. And the joke is that I've devoted my whole goddamn life to it."

I sat there in a state of shock as you poured yourself another drink.

You smiled. "I've shocked you."

"No. Really."

"Well, I'm getting drunk, so I don't care. And I'm tired. And I'd like you to go."

I rose uncertainly to my feet. "Mrs. Norman?"

"What?"

"People do need poetry. I mean, life is so terrible that . . . art is necessary."

"How can life be terrible at eighteen?"

23

"You don't have to be old to suffer," I said.

"No?"

"No."

"And so you think my work matters?"

"Yes! It matters more than I can tell you. To all kinds of people. To me."

You started to laugh. "What's so funny?" I asked.

"Youth—passionate youth. Which is why I stopped teaching. I couldn't keep a straight face."

There was a dull pain inside me and I knew that I had to leave—to force myself to get down the stairs, and go home, and forget you. I knew that I had to save myself before I drowned.

"I have to go now," I said.

"Ah, I've hurt your feelings."

"No, you haven't. But I'll be late for dinner."

"All right. Go. What the hell."

"Don't you want me to go?"

"I don't know what I want," you muttered. "Sleep, maybe. Or to get plastered. I don't know."

I walked to the door, but turned back. "Mrs. Norman?"

"Yes?"

"Could I ask you something?"

"Why not?"

"If poetry doesn't matter to you, why do you still write it every day?"

You grinned at me. "Habit."

24

nine

Christmas vacation came with the sound of church bells and a few ropes of colored lights strung across Main Street. Snow fell endlessly and the river became shrouded and unreal. The little kids went sledding, while the older ones hung out at the new shopping center, five miles north. My father turned jovial and asked my sister and me what we wanted for Christmas. Sally immediately replied, "My own house," and I broke into unfortunate laughter. My mother decorated the tree with ropes of popcorn and little candles, but I couldn't say anything kind about it. I was too involved in myself, wondering if I would ever see you again Hadley, and knowing that the wish to see you again was masochistic. Everything seemed shabby and mean—Christmas decorations on the lawn, carols on the radio—and I longed for the courage to do something wild, destructive, cruel. Then these feelings would disappear, to be replaced by a paralyzing sadness. I assumed that you would be having people out for the holiday, friends from the city, and one night I stole down your driveway to see if there were any extra cars. But there was only your little MG, half buried in snow.

I stood there, realizing that I was jealous of these imaginary people—whoever they were, whenever they might appear—and I knew how crazy this was. I didn't even know you, yet my feelings of possessiveness were as strong as if we were married. With a sense of bewilderment, I realized that I didn't want anyone to visit you, that I wanted you kept inviolate and remote.

A few days later it occurred to me that you would not be having people out for Christmas, that you would sit there alone. How I came to this knowledge I am not sure, but there was something so barren about your life, so bitter and angry, that I could not visualize you celebrating a holiday with anyone. You would sit by the fire and drink gin —and once again, a feeling of pity that I barely understood entered my heart.

On Christmas Eve we always went to a midnight church service, and then to my uncle's house for eggnog. But this time I refused to go, and after a noisy fight with my father, was allowed to stay home. I wandered about the house for a long time, looking at the tree and the presents—and finally I understood why I had stayed behind. I put on my coat and a wool cap, took three dollars from the household money, and walked out into the drifting snow. At the corner of Highgate Road a man was selling wreaths and Christmas trees from the back of a truck, and I bought the biggest wreath he had. A few minutes later I was ringing the ship's bell by your door.

The instant the bell made its loud clang I wanted to run, to disappear, to forget the whole thing. I could see how foolish I looked, standing there with a wreath, and I knew that you would open the door and stare at me with contempt. But then the door swung open and it was too late.

You stood in a thin shaft of light, weaving a little and blinking at me—and thoroughly drunk. Your feet were bare, the plaid bathrobe was soiled, and there was a dish towel wrapped around your left hand. I saw blood coming through the towel and dropped the Christmas wreath in the snow. "Mrs. Norman! What happened?"

"Accident. Broke a glass."

"Are you badly hurt?"

You grinned at me. "Who knows?"

"Look," I said, stepping into the hall, "let's go upstairs and put a bandage on it or something."

"Don't need a bandage."

"Please. You're bleeding very hard."

I followed you upstairs into the living room, where a hurricane seemed to have struck. Plates, glasses, magazines and books were strewn wildly about and in the midst of it all sat Sam, a complacent look on his face. "Do you have any gauze?" I asked.

"In the kitchen."

But the kitchen was even more chaotic than the rest of the house, and it was a long time before I found a small first-aid kit. I came back to the living room and saw that you were lying on the couch, your face turned away from me. "Mrs. Norman?"

"What?"

"I found the first-aid kit."

Trembling with nervousness, I swabbed the cut and made a bandage out of gauze and adhesive tape. It looked amateurish, but at least the bleeding had stopped.

"How do you feel?" I asked.

"Like hell," you said, your face still turned away.

"Well . . . can I get you anything?"

"A drink."

"You've had enough to drink," I said quietly.

After a minute you looked at me. "Do you know something awful?"

"No. What?"

"I'm going to be sick."

I swallowed hard. "All right. Where's the bathroom?"

"I'm disgusting, aren't I?"

"No, it's OK."

I helped you to the bathroom, where you were violently ill, and brought you back to the living room. You were shaking now, and I was frightened, so I said, "Look—let me get you upstairs and into bed. You need sleep." Then my arm was around you, and I was coaxing you up the narrow staircase into the loft. The touch of you was so strange, so foreign and new, that for a moment everything paused and I hovered in time, my arm around your thin shoulders and you leaning heavily against me.

Your bed was a tangle of pillows and blankets, and no sooner had you curled up in the middle of it than I heard Sam at the bottom of the staircase, whimpering. He wanted to be with you, but the stairs were too steep—so I went down and hoisted him under my arm and climbed to the loft again. He leapt into bed beside you, wagged his tail madly, and collapsed in a heap.

28

I went back to the living room and stood in front of the fire. I felt like someone who had inadvertently stumbled into a war, but I knew that I wasn't going to leave. I would stay all night if necessary, and what would happen at home when they found me missing, I didn't contemplate.

I walked about the room picking up glasses and cups, and decided to do the dishes. This took over an hour, since there wasn't a clean dish in the house, and after that I put wood on the fire and straightened up the living room. Your material life, Hadley, was a storm—a whirlwind of unpaid bills and misplaced letters and laundry that never went to the laundromat—and it would take me a long time to understand that your sense of order was reserved for poetry alone. If the furnace broke down in the middle of winter, it stayed broken for weeks. If a windowpane was cracked, you mended it with brown tape and left it that way.

I emptied all the ashtrays and scraped a pile of ashes from the card table where you worked. Then I saw the poem. Half-finished, and written in pencil on a yellow legal pad, it beckoned to me as though it were alive. After a strange little contest with myself—a battle that concerned all kinds of morality—my curiosity won and I took the pad over to the fireplace where there was more light.

I have wondered about insects—the architectural
spider and the delicate moth. I have thought of the
glowworm, lighting its way into birth. Their longevity
stuns my hard bones, and my mind drifts away like a wind.

And fishes too, in their sapphire world, the dark
breathing of gills. I hear them sink down and I know
that they pause there, alive in the deep, alive in
eternity, soft with the swaying of grasses—and
infinite.

The clustering bees will outlive us, and even the
gnats. And the hummingbird pierces the air with no
cry, caught in its amber. Some things live forever,
blinded by stars, and feed on the light. . . .

I did not know what the poem meant, nor why I was
reading it. I did not want to know. And because this was
my first intuition of your fate, pressed hard into my mind
on some subliminal level, I stopped reading and put the
yellow pad back on the table. The words had no relationship to the woman who had just fallen asleep upstairs,
drunk. The words had no meaning at all.

ten

I slept on the couch that night as bells chimed in the distance and tugboats hooted their horns. Snow drifted down
like feathers, delicate and pure, and all the sounds mingled
in my dreams. The fire banked itself into glowing coals,
and at dawn a lone bird began to sing. I woke and saw light
coming through the window, and in the tree beyond, a

blood-red cardinal. I sat up and rubbed my eyes—then turned as I heard you coming down the stairs.

You glanced at me without a hint of surprise and walked into the bathroom, closing the door behind you. After a long while you emerged wearing slacks and a sweater, your face washed, your hair neatly combed. You looked pale as death, but were utterly composed, and without looking at me again brought Sam downstairs, opened a can of dog food for him and plugged in the coffeepot. I kept waiting for you to apologize for the previous night—but not a word came.

At last you came out of the kitchen and said, "Do you want coffee?"

"Yes. Thank you."

You brought out two steaming mugs and placed them on the table near the couch as I put wood on the fire.

"No hangover," you announced.

"No?" I said politely.

"Nope. Sheer luck. Did you put me to bed?"

"Yes."

"I don't remember. Christ—look at the snow. A blizzard. Won't they be missing you at home?"

"I don't know. I hope not."

You collapsed in the easy chair and took a sip of coffee. "I'm sorry, but I don't remember your name. David, was it?"

"Steven."

"Ah, yes. Steven the poet. Did you put this bandage on my hand?"

31

"Yes."

"Well, you're a real Samaritan, aren't you?"

I had no reply, and once again I felt dulled by sadness. I knew that my presence had no meaning for you—that I could have been anyone.

"Do you know something?" you asked.

"No. What?"

"It's Christmas Day."

"Gee—I'd forgotten. How weird."

"Doesn't feel like Christmas, does it?"

I thought of the wreath I had brought you, lying downstairs, and said, "No."

"I suppose we should be drinking eggnog or something. On the other hand, I've always hated holidays. As a child I did my best to spoil them."

"Were you an only child?" I asked.

"Uh huh. And you?"

"I've got a younger sister. Sally."

"And what does your father do?"

"He owns a hardware store—with my uncle."

"And he thinks you're a faggot for writing poetry."

I looked up, stunned. "Well, yes. But he's never used that word."

"Don't worry, he will . . . I have the feeling my language shocks you."

"Yes," I admitted. "It does."

"It used to drive John crazy, but I can't help it."

"Who's John?"

"My ex-husband. From whom I am presently escaping."

I sat there for a moment, trying to absorb this new piece of information. "You mean, that's why you moved up here? Away from the city?"

A look of annoyance passed over your face. "Exactly. Tell me—why did you sleep here last night?"

"To be sure you were OK. I was worried."

"I see. Nobody drinks in your family, I suppose?"

"No. They're sort of straitlaced. My mother's father was a minister, actually."

"How amazing."

"Why?"

You yawned. "No particular reason . . . Well Steven, if you'll excuse me, I've got to get to work."

"On Christmas?" I asked.

"Why not?"

"I don't know. It just seems strange."

You rose quickly to your feet. "Have a good holiday."

"Thank you," I said. And then I took a wild chance. "May I see you again?"

You stared at me. "Whatever for?"

"To . . . well, to talk. There are very few people I can talk to."

"And so you've chosen me?"

I took a deep breath. "Yes."

"I don't know why these things always happen to me. I swear to God I don't."

"What things?"

"Lost cats. Lost dogs. And now lost children. I am not a kind person, as you may have noticed by now, so why does it happen?"

"I don't know," I said miserably.

"All right, Steven. Come back and tell me your troubles. But not for a few days. OK? I've got work to do."

"All right," I said, walking to the door. I stood there for a second, staring at a pile of unopened Christmas cards.

You followed my glance. "I told you I hated holidays."

"Then I'm glad I didn't send you a card!"

You winked at me. "So am I."

An hour later I lay safely in my own bed. My mind was racing and every word we had said to each other was being played over and over, like a tape. I saw you coming down the stairs, your hair a blond tangle. I saw you sitting by the fire sipping coffee. I felt, almost tangibly, the charged atmosphere you lent to a room, your bland acceptance of your fame, your disregard for convention. No, I thought, it was more than that. What I felt was a kind of drunkenness, an indefinable longing, a sense that if I closed my eyes and prayed I could transform the world . . . Suddenly I sat straight up in bed—understanding for the first time that I was in love.

The irony of it hit me. I was in love with a person I did not like.

eleven

It was so strange to be in love, so new. As though I had been sleeping all my life and wakened. As though I had been blind and found sight. Every sense—touch, taste, smell—became reborn, and I moved through the world in a state of wonder. All at once I was seeing *into* things: the flight of a starling against the naked sky, lavender crystals in the snow, the dark arms of winter trees. I saw nature, I saw myself. And everything had meaning.

I walked by the river, watching chunks of ice sail by, and knew that this river wound its way to the Atlantic and that all things were one. I saw a tanker pass and waved wildly to a man on deck—realizing that I had not done such a thing since I was a child. Across the water a tiny train snaked along the shore, and the rhythm of its wheels echoed deep inside me. Sea gulls perched on the ice, their gray and white wings blending with winter, and I felt a sense of joy at their life, and at my own.

Hadley, I could not listen to music without feeling that it connected us. I could not read a poem without knowing that the words were a bridge upon which I would cross to you. Everything beautiful bound you to me—and I believed, without the slightest logic, that the force of my love would enter you like a presence and change your life.

It did not seem odd that I had never loved before, that

no human being had ever reached me. I had lived my life in books, and the only love I had known was fictional, romantic and remote. Love meant poetry to me, and Mahler, and old films on television. And though I had dated a girl for two years in high school, and been infatuated, I had never understood that falling in love is indeed a fall—a crash into a different world.

Drifting, stumbling, dreaming, I waited for three days before I called you—having memorized your phone number that Christmas morning—and when you said that you would join me for a walk, I felt dizzy with happiness. I spent an hour dressing, and at one point Sally came and stood in the doorway and watched. The expression on her face was curious—too wise, too adult—and for a moment I considered telling her about you. Then I reminded myself that she was only twelve years old, grinned at her, and left the house.

twelve

Our feet were crunching on the hard snow and Sam was trotting ahead of us, his tail up like a little flag. The ice-coated branches of trees sparkled in the sunshine and the sky was an extraordinary blue. As yet we had said little to each other, but the joy inside me was so intense that I had no need for words. I glanced briefly at you, loving the ski pants and heavy sweater you wore, the knitted cap on your head. Your face in the sunlight had a translucent quality, and I wondered why I had not found you beautiful when we first met.

"Cat got your tongue?" you asked.

"No. Not really."

"What then?"

"I don't know. I was just thinking."

"About what?"

"Ezra Pound," I said, surprising myself.

"OK. What about Ezra Pound?"

I hesitated—knowing that I was inventing a topic, yet interested all the same. "Well . . . I was just wondering what you thought about him being locked up in a mental hospital. I mean, what's your opinion of it?"

You gave me a cold look. "Do you know that that is the kind of question that bores the hell out of me?"

"I'm sorry," I said, feeling the color rise to my face.

"Don't be sorry. But really, Steven, who cares?"

"I do."

"Why?"

"Because he's a great poet."

"He broadcast for the Fascists during the Second War."

"So what?"

"So *what*? He committed treason."

"Well, I don't think that has anything to do with art," I declared.

"What makes you think that good artists are good people?"

"Pound is . . ."

"Pound is a crazy old man who hates Jews. As far as I know, they were perfectly right to lock him up. He's free now anyway, so what's the point?"

"The point is that he's a great poet!"

"He is not a great poet," you said. "A linguist, yes. And a brilliant translator. But the word 'great' has to be reserved for innovators—those who break new ground."

"Like you?" I asked.

"Yes," you replied without batting an eyelash. "Like me."

This silenced me for a while and we walked deeper into the woods. I wondered how you could be so egotistical—and then I wondered if egotism was not, perhaps, necessary to survival. After a few moments you said, "You know, real writers, working writers, are different from what you think."

"In what sense?"

"In the sense that they are not special, or beautiful, or deep. God—most of the time they aren't even *nice*. Read the biographies. Alcoholism, paranoia, insane promiscuity, wild selfishness."

"What about Rilke?"

"Rilke was an esthete who deserted a wife and child and spent most of his time living off rich women."

"That isn't true."

"Of course it's true. And Hart Crane committed suicide. And Robert Frost mistreated his family. And Vincent Millay—as she loved calling herself—was really a drunk and a fraud. Why should you worship writers when there have been people in the world like Jesus and Buddha?"

"Then what's the point of art?"

You stopped walking and leaned against a tree. "I have no idea. Except that it's a legal way of working out one's madness. Can we sit down somewhere? I'm out of breath."

I looked around and saw a large tree that had fallen in the woods. We sat down on it and I noticed that you were very pale.

"No wind," you said with a smile. "Would you believe that I used to be a hockey star?"

I laughed. "No."

"Well, I was. In preparatory school. All the girls envied me."

"Private school?"

"Uh huh."

"Sounds nice."

"It was. We all wore school blazers and recited Shelley and got crushes on the teachers. My special crush was a woman named Miss Murdock who taught drama and had holes in her stockings."

"Were you writing in those days?"

"As a kid? Oh, yes. Madly. I wrote poems and stories from the time I was eight years old . . . You know what makes me angry?"

"No. What?"

"The fact that most people think writers are rich and only work a few hours a day. Well, I've published ten books and can barely pay my rent. Don't look so shocked. It's true."

"But how can it be true?"

"The average earnings of the American writer are three thousand dollars a year. Most of us are eligible for welfare. And the painters are worse off than that. And the actors starve—literally. So why do people envy artists?"

I paused, trying to analyze why I envied artists. "I think it's because . . . well, because artists achieve identity. And because they leave their work behind them. You know? A kind of immortality."

"Very profound."

"Well, that's what I think it is."

"Well, *I* think this is a stupid conversation."

"I'm sorry," I said, wounded.

"Do stop saying you're sorry about everything. It's just that art is a boring topic to me. Come on. Let's go home."

We followed our footsteps back through the forest as the sun lowered and branches cast blue shadows on the snow. A terrible sadness swept over me as I realized that the day was ending.

"What are you thinking about?" you asked.

"Pound," I lied. "He *was* an innovator."

Abruptly you turned into an English teacher. "He was an instigator, Steven. He started important movements like Imagism, and he was a great benefactor of other poets, but he was not an innovator. As a matter of fact, his largest body of work is a mess. The *Cantos*."

"Then who would you consider a great poet?"

"Gerard Manley Hopkins," you said quietly. "Who tried to find God."

When we reached your house the sun was gone entirely. A chill had fallen over the woods and the tops of fir trees moved slightly in the wind. You picked up Sam, and hoisted him under your arm. "This has been nice, Steven. I've enjoyed it."

And in those polite words I heard "Good-bye." Speak, I said to myself, speak quickly. Or you will never see her again. "Mrs. Norman . . ."

"Well?"

"Maybe we could do this again."

"Do what?"

"Take a walk. Discuss things. I'd really like to."

"I'm sure you would. But I don't have much time these days. I'm working on a book."

"Oh. Well—that's too bad. I'd really enjoy seeing you again."

You stared me straight in the eye. "Forgive the bluntness, Steven, but that's your problem."

I stood there for a long moment, and to my horror I realized that you were still staring at me—calmly and casually—waiting to see what would happen. For a second I despised you, and then something in me changed. "Mrs. Norman, I need to see you again. It's life or death."

"Why?"

"Because there's no one in the whole world I can talk to. And I've never shown my poetry to a soul. I keep sending it to magazines and it keeps coming back with rejection slips, and sometimes I want to kill myself."

You shook your head. "Ah, Steven . . ."

"I mean it. There are times I don't want to live."

"Don't say such a stupid thing! You're at the very beginning of your life. And why, in the name of Christ, should they accept your poems?"

"Would you read them?"

"I told you. I don't read the work of . . ."

"Please."

"Do you know why I came to this godforsaken town? To be alone. To work. To not have to look at a single human being. And now you crash into my life with all the subtlety of an elephant, asking me to teach you how to write."

"I know how to write, but I don't have a reader! There's nobody to read my work."

"What about your English teacher?"

"Mrs. Norman, my English teacher is an ass."

You burst into laughter. "All right, all right, all right. God save me from the young. All right! Come New Year's Day. But I warn you—I'm tough."

"So am I," I said with newfound boldness. "Good night."

thirteen

On New Year's Eve I sat in my room with the lights out and gazed at the sky: a field of velvet swarming with icy stars. My parents were at my uncle's house, and though Jerry had phoned to invite me to a party, I had turned him down. "What's the matter with you these days?" he had asked irritably—and I had had no reply. If I couldn't be with you on New Year's, Hadley, I wanted to be alone. To remember and recreate you. To hold you in my mind.

I tried to put the pieces of you together like a puzzle. Humor and bitterness. Gentleness spoiled by anger. Egotism. Vanity. A sense of God. How could so many opposites be reconciled within one person? And yet there were moments when I felt you as a single entity—as a soul, perhaps—and it was at these moments that I loved you most. Somewhere inside you was a radiance, a source of light that illumined the darkest place in me.

There was only one problem, and by now it was a strange one: in your presence I felt completely unnatural. The person I was at home—a boy easily provoked to anger, moody, and constantly accused of being selfish—vanished into thin air the moment I saw you. And, though highly vocal with other people, I could no more have protested your constant rudeness to me than flown to the moon. I understand the cause of this paralysis now, which was simply a fear of losing you, but in those days it baffled me and made me miserable. I wanted you to see me as a romantic figure—dark and somewhat mysterious—and wound up acting like a child. Each time we met I would plan the occasion in advance, like a scenario, only to have the play collapse the minute you opened your mouth. You would never say the right lines and I could never abandon my self-consciousness—turning each meeting into a secret disaster. Back home again, I would stare in the mirror at my wild curly hair and small nose, the slightly sensual mouth, and wonder how you saw them—if there was anything about them that was attractive. Then I would realize, with a sense of grief, that you didn't notice these things, that your attention was inward.

What was it really, to be in love? A strange intoxication mixed with pain, or a mysterious sense that one was incorporating the other person into oneself? Days after seeing you, your presence still clung to me and I felt bathed in your aura like warm rain. In ways that I could not understand I wanted to become you, to shed my old self and take on all of your beauty. Our ages, our sexes—these were hardly relevant. I wanted to be reborn as a person named Hadley Norman and enter my life through a new door.

I sat gazing at the sky and saw the stars swim away, drifting outward into the winter night. At twelve o'clock, the man next door ran out on his porch and blew a toy trumpet to celebrate the New Year. For some reason this foolish action made me ache with loneliness, and for a second I

44

considered going into the next room and waking my sister. What I longed to say was: Sally, I am in love. And the person I love is only a few blocks away from here. She is not a nice person—maybe not even a good one—but she is the only thing on earth that can bring me peace. Sally, I am in love, but this woman dwells so far beyond me, in a world so different from the one I know, that I feel like a fool when I am with her and bereft when I am not. Help me, lead me, tell me what to do. . . .

I went into the next room and stood by Sally's bed, but didn't wake her. Because in that bed was simply a twelve-year-old who was sleeping the deep sleep of a child, who clutched a pillow and whose face was tearstained from some recent argument. I gazed at her tangled brown hair and small clenched fists and felt very old—very far away —realizing for the first time that childhood is a country that admits no foreigners.

fourteen

My sister, hitchhiking now through the vastness of America, remember me. While you eat in diners and joke with people you do not know. While you and your friends sleep along the highway, wrapped in army blankets and ponchos. While you smoke grass, inhaling the sweetness of your lives from good stuff or bad stuff, bought at random and used at random. My sister, remember me. When you make love with strangers. When you stroll through the neon cities of car lots and drive-ins. When you gaze at the shanty towns of the South, the wildness of the Rockies, the desert, and Big Sur. "I'm going to Monterey," you said, "or maybe Taos. I don't know. Somewhere. Someplace." And so you vanished like a dandelion, blown higher and higher on the wind. Like the small petal of a flower. Like the memory of a child I had known—long ago.

fifteen

We stood in front of the fireplace on New Year's Day, facing each other, and it flashed through my mind that this was going to be a contest. It was obvious that you had a hangover, and you were wearing the plaid bathrobe, which by now I had come to hate. The poems in my hand felt as heavy as lead, and for a second I had the peculiar sensation that my fingers were stuck to them. "Here they are," I said, handing you the manila folder.

"Fine," you said impatiently. "Now please absent yourself."

"Excuse me?"

"Take Sam for a walk or something. I can't read with you looking over my shoulder."

"OK. Where should I go?"

46

"How should I know? Across the river and into the trees. Anywhere."

I took Sam's leash from the table by the door. "When would you like me to come back?"

"That, my dear boy, depends on how good the work is," you said, curling up on the couch.

A few minutes later Sam and I stood outdoors, gazing at each other. The expression on his face was quizzical and it made me want to laugh. "Come on, Sam," I said, and as we started down the lane he glanced at me over his shoulder and gave an encouraging woof.

There were ten neatly typed poems in the manila folder, and the moment I had handed them to you, my confidence had evaporated. There was definitely something wrong with me, I decided, because one minute I thought my work was beautiful, and the next I felt it had no value at all. In addition to which, the mood you were in was not favorable to the reading of anyone's work—amateur or professional. "Dear God," I said suddenly, "If you will let her like the poems, I'll do anything you want. If you will just let her like them, I'll change my whole life." And, at that particular moment, the fact that I did not believe in God was irrelevant.

After a half hour of aimless walking, I turned back to the house. Sam was straining at the leash, wanting to get home, and before opening the front door, I took a deep breath. "I'm back!" I called, bounding up the stairs.

You were standing by the window with a drink in your

47

hand, and my heart sank as I saw the expression on your face. It was one of total irritation—anger mixed with weariness—and I knew at once that I was in for a bad time.

"You . . . didn't like them," I said.

"Sit down," you replied. "And, if humanly possible, be quiet."

I took off my coat, sat down on the couch and waited.

"Now to begin with—what you have shown me is not the work of a person named Steven Harper. It is, instead, a very clever imitation of the early poems of Rainer Maria Rilke. So criticism is impossible."

"But . . ."

"What's more," you stated calmly, "there is not a single experience in these poems which you have had yourself. They're all mixed up with death and tragedy and metaphysics, and are therefore unspeakably dull."

"Mrs. Norman . . ."

"I'm not finished. The third point I want to make is that you are too old to indulge yourself this way. Imitation is for high school students doing English assignments. If you want to be a poet, you'll have to scrap all this pretentiousness and start from the beginning."

"What would you consider the beginning?" I asked.

"Yourself," you replied. And with that, you turned on your heel and walked into the kitchen.

I did not know what I felt at that moment: shock, bewilderment or pain. All I knew was that my whole world had collapsed within the space of a few sentences, a few casual words.

You emerged from the kitchen with a fresh drink and went to sit by the fire. "Well?"

"Isn't there anything good about them?"

"Not a single thing. They're dreadful."

I rose to my feet. "Well, then. I'd better go."

"What for?"

"What *for*? You've just told me that my work stinks, that it's dreadful."

"Oh, be quiet and sit down," you said wearily. "I'm not finished."

I sat down again, anger flaring inside me like a wound. "Tell me," you said after a moment. "Why do you admire Rilke so much?"

I stared at the floor. "I don't know. Because he's not like anyone else, I guess."

"Exactly."

"Do you like the *Duino Elegies?*" I asked.

"Yes. They're beautiful poems. But the reason they're beautiful is that Rilke closed his eyes and looked into the darkness of himself before he began to write. And that's what you will have to do before you write a single word that's good."

"But I thought you said I had no talent!"

"I never said that. What I said was that these particular poems are imitations, and therefore dreadful. It seems to me that anyone who can imitate Rilke's style as cleverly as you do has, probably, a good deal of talent. But you've never used it."

"Then how do I use it? What do I do?"

49

"Well, there isn't a formula—if that's what you want. The only way to become a writer is to write. Every day. All of your life."

"But I do!"

"What you do every day, my dear, is spend languid hours imitating poets greater than yourself. What I would like to see from you is something of your own, something personal."

"OK," I said fiercely. "OK. I'll try. I mean, all this is really very helpful."

You began to laugh, and when I asked why you were laughing, you said, "Because you sound like something out of Salinger."

"You don't like Salinger?"

"I *despise* Salinger. But since he is very popular with the young, I try to keep quiet about it. . . . Tell me, Steven, could you be happy if you didn't write? If circumstances prevented you?"

"No, never. I'd die."

"Which probably means that you will be a writer. Well, don't look so happy about it. It's nothing to anticipate."

"You keep saying that."

"Look. To begin with, the glow of being a writer wears off very soon. Almost as soon as you've seen your name in print a few times. Then there's the money, which is laughable—and the loneliness, which is vast. *Then* there are the critics, who praise you for the wrong things and damn you for the wrong things, leaving you to realize that no one

50

understands your writing except yourself. But the real trouble is that the deeper you get into work, the more you discover your ignorance. And the more you discover your ignorance, the more you seek knowledge. Until—if you're any good at all—you wind up compulsive and driven and totally self-involved. Like me."

I waited a few seconds, and then I asked, "Do you really feel you have wasted your life?"

"Yes. I do."

"But why! You've had things that other people—people like me—would give everything for. Fame and prestige and ten books published, and . . ."

"Oh, Steven, you're talking like a child. I can't believe that you're this innocent. Do you know the price I've had to pay for my talent? Complete loneliness. The inability to love. An unwillingness to do anything that would distract from my work. As a result of which, I have no friends, no lovers, and no family. A hell of a picture to look at in one's middle age."

"But it was worth it, wasn't it?"

"I don't know."

"It must have been!"

You rose to your feet. "I'm getting tired, so I think this interview should end. Come back on Tuesday with two new poems. Your *own* poems."

I blinked. "Excuse me?"

"I said, come back on Tuesday and we'll try again. Not that I think writing can be taught. But I may be able to help you avoid some pitfalls. The way you're going now, it will be twenty years before you achieve anything. And," you said absently, "life is short."

"Mrs. Norman?"

"What?"

"I don't know how to thank you."

"Then don't," you said. "Gratitude's a bore."

sixteen

It made no sense to me: the fact that you had taken me on as a pupil. It seemed too good to be true, and I couldn't fathom the reason for it. You had stated that you needed to be alone, that you were finishing a book, that you were not a kind person. Yet from that day on you tutored me twice a week, going over my work with the meticulousness of a jeweler, criticizing, explaining, lecturing. I couldn't believe my luck—yet at the same time I suffered the tortures of the damned.

"If you're going to work with me, you'd better forget your sensitivities," you said—and I soon learned that you meant this literally. You were cruel in your criticism of my poems, uncompromising in your demands, and if I had ever thought that poetry was written by inspiration, I was to change my mind. You required two poems a week from me whether I felt like writing or not, and the analysis of these poems was a graduate course in itself. It was unbelievable how much you knew about literature—and how intolerant you were of other writers. Nobody's work was any good, whether his name was T. S. Eliot or William Butler Yeats, and the ease with which you dismissed geniuses absolutely stunned me. Yeats was a "sentimental fool," Eliot a "timid bank clerk," and Amy Lowell a "fat Sapphist." Edna St. Vincent Millay, whom you particularly loathed, was referred to as "that alcoholic." And because I had never known an artist before, I did not realize that such fierce competitiveness, with both the living and the dead, was a mark of fame.

The contemporary poets—Sylvia Plath, W. S. Merwin, Adrienne Rich—were dismissed by you as not knowing their craft. And so, with a few peculiar exceptions like Edith Sitwell ("She has a sense of humor.") the world of literature was decimated as though by a bomb. On the other hand, extravagant words of praise for minor poets would sometimes escape your lips, confusing me utterly and making me realize that as far as other writers were concerned your opinions were not objective.

I stopped thinking about being published and I stopped thinking about the glamour of art. I stopped thinking, as a matter of fact, about anything except writing two poems a week that would reflect my own life. You wrote until three every afternoon, and I would usually arrive a half hour later and take Sam for a walk while you read my work. Then we would sit in front of the fire and talk until dinnertime.

It gave me such joy to be part of your life, to know your

53

schedule and habits, to carry in the box of groceries that arrived each day at three-thirty. It gave me such secret pleasure to know exactly when you would go to the kitchen for coffee, when you would run out of cigarettes, and I began to do errands for you like picking up your dry cleaning or taking parcels to the post office. I guess I was trying to impose order on your life even then, Hadley—carrying cups and glasses into the kitchen, emptying the ashtrays— but your sense of discipline was reserved for poetry alone. You rose at seven o'clock, had breakfast, and worked until midafternoon with exactly one half hour off for lunch. You did not answer the phone during those hours, or do chores, and the whole pattern seemed so extreme that one day I asked you about it. You shrugged. "I don't know. It's simply a way to get the work done."

"How do you mean?"

"Well . . . writing is rather like a mined field in a war: it's filled with hidden work blocks that can explode in your face. A sudden sense of fear, a sense of failure. A terror that once you get into the subconscious there may be nothing there. So you overcome these blocks by paying the work great respect. Do you understand?"

"No. Not really."

"You have to make the work terribly important so the mind will open up. You have to go to the desk each day and punch that imaginary time clock and put in your hours —even if nothing comes. And God knows, there are whole weeks when nothing comes."

"But don't many writers work by inspiration?"

You flashed me an irritable look. "No, goddammit. Why do people always think that? No writer worth his salt sits around waiting to be inspired. He simply gets to that table rain or shine, hangover or no hangover, and puts in his hours. And since that kind of behavior is very seductive to the work, the work eventually pays him back."

"It's all so different from what people think," I said lamely.

"So is everything," you replied. And the subject was closed.

In view of conversations like this, it came as a shock to me to learn that you relied on pills as well as liquor to get through your life—and that you lied about both. "For headaches," you would say, as you swallowed a pink and white capsule. "The first drink of the day," you would announce cheerfully—when I knew it was your third. And so my admiration for you was constantly being challenged, and sometimes when you were high I experienced despair. It was as if you had stepped away into a little world of your own, a cosy place where you had particular secrets and enjoyed particular jokes. A glazed look would come into your eyes then, and your language would get worse than usual. Four-letter words abounded, causing me strange grief, and accusations bubbled to the top of your mind like champagne. Your ex-husband had been a bastard. Your publisher was a thief. Your agent should be "institutionalized."

Since I knew very well that pills and liquor didn't mix, I decided to be bold one day and mention it. "Listen," you said slowly, "just mind your own business."

"But Mrs. Norman—it isn't safe."

"What the hell do you know about it?"

"Not very much, but . . ."

"Then shut up. It's none of your business."

"I only mentioned it because . . ."

"I said: shut up."

"I'm sorry," I mumbled.

"OK, OK. Let's get back to work."

You ran a hand impatiently through your hair and looked around for your drink. And I saw that the plaid bathrobe had cigarette burns in it now, and that one of the pockets was torn. I saw that your eyes had circles under them, as though you had had no sleep, and that your lips were dry and parched.

"Mrs. Norman? I'm sorry I brought it up. Really."

"Oh, Steven, you're using your *Salinger* voice again."

I sat there looking at you, loving and hating you all at once, blind as to why you were destroying yourself, wanting to save you—and feeling a million miles away. Hadley, it was so wrong of you not to tell me.

You had cancer. And pills and liquor dulled the pain.

seventeen

My old life was fading away. Slowly, almost invisibly, my direction had changed. I lived in my parents' house, went to school, talked to people—but the boy who did these

56

things was a ghost. Jerry vanished from the scene as though I had never known him and began running with a new crowd. Sally battled her small way through the world, fighting with my father, rebelling against rules, and still I saw nothing. I was like a dreamer among the dead, a puppet who went through the motions of life without feeling them. Slowly, imperceptibly, I was becoming a poet. And slowly, you were beginning to notice my love.

It happened in little ways: our hands touching by accident, a sudden smile between us, a sudden silence. "She knows," I would say to myself—and then, "She doesn't know." I skirted the borders of your life like one who cannot tell if he is enemy or friend. I threw out hints and took them back. "She knows," my mind kept whispering. And then, "She doesn't know." And always the phrase "I love you" thundering like an ocean in my mind, spinning and tossing its wheel of colored lights, hurting my throat with its silence. I love you, I love you. I love. Inflections changing, halting, the phrase about to be spoken—then taken back. I love you, Hadley, but cannot tell you. I love you, and you do not know.

Why am I a fool with you? Silent when I would speak, and talkative when there should be silence? Why am I caught so terribly between wanting to reveal myself, and some unnamed fear? Inside me rage a hundred people— men and women, children, lovers—but I can show none of them to you, and in bewilderment I watch them endlessly retreat, marching the hills of my mind. If I could show you—only once—who I am, I would know peace.

Come into my soul dressed in white. Come with flowers. Come close to me and see me as I am.

I will make poems for you and place the smoke of steamers flat against the air. I will throw a net over a bay and capture it like a bright blue fish—pin far sails to the horizon. And the tall sea-grass will not yield to the wind, and the cry of the gulls will rest high.

Come into my soul with flowers, roses and anemones. Walk into my eyes and stand in their pools. Sunlight and shadow, sapphire evenings, deep grass.

The song holds us both.

eighteen

I stood by the door putting on Sam's leash, and you said, "Don't stay out long. It's raining."

"Who are you worried about? Sam or me?"

"Sam, of course. He's very prone to colds."

You lay down on the couch with the manila folder I had brought you. I wrote four this week," I said.

"Four poems? Goodness. How productive you are."

"Well," I said, my spirits fading, "so long. I'll be back soon."

Sam looked at me as though I were crazy to take him for a walk, but we went outdoors nonetheless, shivering in the February rain. The woods had a smell of spring—ice melting, bulbs preparing to grow—and as my thoughts returned to you a dreadful loneliness filled my heart. It seemed as if we had known one another forever, and not at all. As if we were intimate, and strangers. And the attraction I felt between us came and went like the wind. Some days you would be playful and flirtatious with me, but on other occasions I felt only that I irritated you and that you would have given anything to shut me out of your life.

Once, walking together in the woods, you had stumbled and I had grabbed you to keep you from falling—and in that instant I had believed that we felt the same. Our eyes had met and you had searched my face, looking for the answer to a question no one had asked, but then you had pulled back and the moment was gone. I remember the deliberate way you trudged on down the path, your voice animated and bright, your gestures telling me that I meant nothing to you. . . . Moments like these were a kind of exquisite torture, and whenever we collided by accident I felt as if I had been brushed with fire.

I tried to ask myself what I wanted from you—but could not find the answer. I asked myself what I wanted most in the world, and did not know. Some days it seemed that one kind word from you would make me happy. Other times, I wanted so terribly to touch you that my hands shook. But you were as remote as a figure carved in ice. Light shone from you—and I could not enter the circle of its brilliance.

Back at the house, I took off my muddy boots and went

into the kitchen to get some coffee. You were lying on the couch with your eyes closed and I thought you were asleep. Then you said, "Bring me some coffee too. OK?"

"Sure," I said, getting another mug. "Did you read them all?"

"Yes. I read them."

I gave you your coffee and sat down in the easy chair, but you said nothing more. Finally I asked, "Well?"

You sat up on one elbow. "You worry me sometimes, Steven. Did you know that?"

"No, I didn't. How come?"

"Because you're so goddamn earnest. Holden Caulfield writing poetry."

"I'm sorry."

"If you say you're sorry one more time I'll throw this coffee at you."

"OK, OK. But I *am* sorry."

"I just wish you'd relax, that's all. You make me nervous."

"Oh."

"Well, you do. I'm even beginning to see your tense little face in my dreams. There it sits: brow furrowed, eyes glazed, waiting for me to say something brilliant You put a great burden on me."

"I'm sorr . . . Oh, never mind."

"You've got years in which to become a writer. It doesn't have to be done overnight."

"I don't get it," I said. "I really don't."

"Get what?"

"You make me work like a maniac and then you tell me I've got years. I just don't get it."

"You find me arbitrary?"

"Yes!"

"Well, perhaps I am. One of the advantages of age. Would you hand me the pills on the card table?"

"Mrs. Norman . . ."

"I said, hand me the pills, Steven. You're not my keeper."

I watched as you took two pills and swallowed them with coffee. "By the way," you said casually, "one of the poems in this folder is lovely. The first good thing you've done."

Why did you wait this long to tell me? I thought. Why are you so cruel? Then the joy of your words flooded me. "Really! Which one? The sonnet?"

"No, the one called *Song*. I'll read it."

"You don't have to read it aloud."

"Why not?" you asked, opening the folder.

"I'd rather you didn't."

"Don't be so silly."

"Actually . . ." I said. But you had already begun.

Bird, upon this single dawn be still,
And use the trembling air
To place a silence on the sky
More beautiful and deathless than a song.

Small bird, within the branches
Wait for light as if no light had been before,
And spread your wings in statue's flight.
Immovable, serene, your softness hold
Within a core curved only to itself.

Dark bird, withhold your deepest song
And blinding stillness bring,
That hers, mounting from a long hushed throat
May sing.

"Now," you said briskly, "the reason I like this one is because it's real. The form's clumsy, of course, but that doesn't matter. The point is that you seem to have written it for someone you love—some girl, perhaps—and that gives it truth."

Silence hung in the air like mist hovering about a mountain. Clouds and sunlight flashed through my mind, wildflowers, soft rain. "I wrote it for you," I said.

"I beg your pardon?"

"I . . . wrote it for you."

You sat up on the couch and ran a hand through your hair. You lit a cigarette and gazed at me. "Well, I guess the time has come for me to make my speech."

"What speech?"

"The one about young boys getting crushes on older women. It's rather boring, so I'll abbreviate it by saying that such things happen all the time and that they're rarely

62

of consequence. The boy always gets over it and—after being momentarily flattered—the woman gives a sigh of relief and goes back to her life. So that's that."

I forced myself to look at you. "You think this is a 'crush,' Mrs. Norman?"

"Absolutely."

"Then I guess you don't know me very well."

"Nobody knows anybody very well."

"That isn't true."

"Of course it is."

I rose to my feet. "I'd better go."

"Oh, Steven, you're always making these dramatic exits. I wish to God you were twenty years older—we might have been friends."

"Aren't we friends now?" I asked.

"Certainly not. Friendship implies equality."

Nothing will ever hurt you as much as this, I told myself. This is the worst that can happen. Go home and forget her. Leave. Force yourself to leave.

I crossed to the door. "I'm going now, Mrs. Norman."

"Fine—it's getting late."

"Shall I come back next week?"

"If you want to. It's immaterial to me."

"Then I guess I won't."

"All right."

"Do you know how cruel you are?" I burst out.

To my amazement, you gave a loud laugh. "I certainly do. My husband used to tell me about it all the time."

nineteen

I sat through dinner that night in silence, skipped dessert and went to my room. I opened a book of short stories and tried to read. And suddenly the grief inside me was so profound that I felt that I would die.

I lay down on the bed and drew the covers over me, unable to move, paralyzed by sadness, and certain that I would never see you again. I heard my own voice asking, "Shall I come back next week?" and your voice replying, "If you want to. It's immaterial to me."

It went round and round in my mind. Shall I come back next week? If you want to. It's immaterial to me. Shall I come back? If you want to. It's immaterial. I saw the hostility in your face, your eyes averted, and wondered how you could be so cruel. . . . Then, without moving, without even a flash of recognition, I understood that you had not meant those words—that you had meant their opposite. I understood that your attitude came from some pain of your own, the cause of which I might never know, but which mysteriously I might heal. I understood that you were more alone on this earth than I was, more desolate, and totally lacking in hope. The bravado, the sarcasm, the feigned indifference to emotion: all were signals for help.

I do not know how I stumbled into this knowledge, Hadley, but it had the feel of absolute truth—so I threw on my jacket, went down the back stairs of our house, and outdoors. It was nine o'clock and within a few minutes I was gazing at your windows.

I opened the front door and stole up the stairs, seeing what I expected to see: Sam asleep on the rug and you sitting in front of the fire with a drink in your hand. What I had not expected to see was the expression on your face—a look of such terrible sadness that my heart moved within me. "Hadley?" I said, and you turned in surprise.

Our eyes met, and I walked over to you and knelt, and put my arms around you. You held onto me hard, and for a moment there was no sound save our breathing. Then I kissed you and touched your soft hair, and felt the world slipping away as you kissed me back. It was as if two needs had finally opened to one another. Not people at first, but needs—your need for life and strength, and mine for all the worlds I had never known. I locked my arms around your waist and kissed you again and again, wanting to drown in you, to become you, to mix your blood with mine.

You pulled away from me and shook your head. "This is madness."

"No," I said, "no."

"Steven . . ."

"I need you."

"No. It's crazy."

Your words faded as I embraced you again—and now we were kissing deeply, locked into one another, our

65

tongues exploring each other's mouths. "Please," I whispered, "please, Hadley. Please."

"No. You don't understand . . ."

"But I do. Please."

"We must stop."

"No. Let me. Please. Come upstairs."

"It's ridiculous. People would find it . . ."

"It doesn't matter."

"But you're a child."

"I need you!"

I was kissing your hands, and your eyes, and stroking your hair—blind with my need of you, the world fallen away into darkness, the universe gone silent save for the words in my mind, all nature stopped in its motion, the planets fixed and immovable, animals, fish and birds, caught forever as in a tapestry.

All life came to a halt. "Please," I said.

At last you nodded, your eyes closed, and leaning against me went up the stairs to the loft. Like someone dazed, you threw off your clothes—slacks and sweater and undergarments—and faced me.

"What's wrong, Steven?"

"I . . ."

"What's wrong?"

"Nothing."

"But there is."

"No. I . . ."

"Tell me."

But I couldn't tell you. Nor could I look at you: t/
whiteness, and the beauty of your breasts and sh(
the delicate whiteness, as of birch trees in winter. I
of snow and silence. Dawn.

"You're not a virgin?" you said softly.

"Yes."

"Why didn't you tell me?"

"I couldn't."

You walked over to me and touched my cheek. "Well
then, we must be very gentle with you."

"I can't . . . I won't be any good."

"Doesn't matter."

"It does!"

"Come to bed, Steven."

"I . . ."

"Come," you said, unbuttoning my shirt. "It's time."

twenty

I could hear a clock ticking in the darkness. A small clock,
its voice ticking away the hours. Rain fell insistently on
the slate roof over our heads and my life seemed far away.
You reached across the bed and took my hand—and I felt
hot tears spring to my eyes.

"Why are you crying, Steven?"

"I'm not."

"Yes, you are. Why?"

"No reason."

"Tell me."

"You know why."

You moved closer to me. "It's never perfect the first time. Didn't you know that?"

"No."

"Well, it isn't. What do you think people do? Just tumble into bed with each other?"

I buried my face in the pillow, unable to speak. Then I felt your arms around me. "What a silly you are. Lovemaking is the greatest art in the world—and here you expect to learn it all at once."

"I wasn't any good," I said into the pillow.

"Well, I hardly think we're engaged in a contest," you replied.

"I wanted to make you happy."

"What nonsense! You make me happy by being here. By being in this bed."

I turned over and looked at you. "Really?"

"Yes, really. You must stop reading novels—they've given you all the wrong information."

"About what?"

"Sex. People in novels always *perform* so well sexually. Whereas life is quite different. Why have you never had a girl?"

I hesitated for a moment. "Because I was afraid."

"Well, you have nothing to be afraid of, absolutely nothing. You're charming in bed. And your body is beautiful."

I stared at you. "It is?"

"Of course it is! Women will go mad for you when you're older."

But I don't want any women, I thought. I only want you. For the rest of my life. "Hadley?" I said. "Can I ask you something?"

"Of course."

"Why are you named Hadley?"

You laughed. "Because I was conceived in a hotel in South Hadley, Massachusetts."

"Oh. . . . But how did they know you were conceived there? Your parents, I mean."

"I haven't the slightest idea."

"Were they writers?"

"God, no. My father was an investment counselor, and my mother was a kind of beautiful dilettante. She grew prize roses and took sculpture classes at night. You know?"

"No. Not really."

"They had money, Steven. Which makes them different from you and me. People with money are very different."

"Didn't they leave you any?" I asked.

"What a lovely question. No dear, they didn't. My father disinherited me when I was just about your age."

"Why?"

"Because I was rebellious. Wild. I refused to go to Smith, Mother's alma mater, and flew off to New York instead. A publisher was interested in my work, and I was involved with a married man, and . . . all kinds of things."

"Did you ever make up with them? Your parents."

69

"No. They wanted to, but I never would. I'm rather a stubborn person, as you may have noticed."

"You mean you never saw them again?"

"Nope. Except for one time when Mother was in the hospital. I was a very black sheep, Steven. The family was glad to be rid of me."

"That's sort of sad."

You leaned over and kissed me. "No, it isn't. Do you want to make love again?"

"Yes."

"The same way?"

"Yes."

"Then slowly this time. And let me help you. All right?"

"All right. Hadley?"

"What?"

"I lo . . ."

"No," you said, covering my mouth with your hand. "Don't say 'I love you.' It's bad luck."

twenty-one

Dawn came into the room with pale gray light, and now there was only a soft dripping of rain on the roof—like fingertips drumming. Somewhere in the distance a rooster crowed, and you raised your head from my chest. "I've been asleep," you said.

"Me too," I replied.

"I wonder what time it is?"

"Dawn," I said, pulling you close to me.

"Silly. Dawn isn't a time."

"Yes, it is."

You yawned. "We haven't had enough sleep. Listen—won't they miss you at home?"

"Not before eight. That's when I come downstairs to catch the bus. I never eat breakfast."

"You should. It's the most important meal of the day."

For some reason this struck us as being funny, and we began to laugh. "Why are we laughing?" I said.

"I don't know."

I clutched you tightly to me. "Do I make you happy? Please say yes."

"Yes. A million times."

"It was nice, wasn't it? Better, I mean."

"Yes, darling. It was nice."

I buried my face in your neck. "Oh, Hadley."

"What? What is it?"

"You never said 'Darling' before."

"You never gave me a chance."

"Is this what people mean by happiness?"

You stroked my hair. "Yes. I think so."

"Because I've never been happy before. Have you?"

You paused for only the briefest second, and then you said, "No."

"I wish I didn't have school today."

"Well, you do, so that's that. And I must work. . . . Do you want to come for supper tonight?"

71

"Yes."

"I'm a lousy cook."

"It doesn't matter. I'll come. And I'll bring wine or something. And flowers!"

You gazed at me. "I'm not sure I can handle all this, you know."

"All what?"

"You. Your youth."

"Hadley . . . if all we ever had was last night, it would still be enough. I mean, nothing has ever been so beautiful for me."

"All right," you said gently. "All right."

twenty-two

I came back at seven o'clock—having told my mother that I was going out with friends—and found you lying on the couch with Sam, asleep. The bottle of gin was nearby, but somehow it didn't bother me. Nothing could have bothered me that night because I had spent the whole day in a state of rapturous joy. The experience I had waited for all my life had finally come to me in a shower of gold. And it was not what I anticipated. Not lust or conquest—but a plunge into a world of things unnameable, echoes that struck half-remembered chords of music, reverberations that opened a door into my soul. And suddenly I was glad that I had never slept with anyone before, profoundly glad, because it was you who had given these things to me—and now, no matter what happened, they could not be erased.

I walked into your house that night with a bottle of wine and six roses. At the last minute I had also purchased a tiny bottle of perfume, and so I deposited these gifts on the card table and went to kneel by your side.

"Hadley?"

"Ummm?"

"It's me. I'm here."

We began to kiss—shyly, as though we had never kissed before—touching each other, murmuring words and hearing words, Sam staring at us in surprise and logs sputtering on the fire, the night gone silent and cold, and the house very still. I felt as if a hundred years had passed since we had made love.

"After dinner," you said smiling.

"Before. Please."

"*After,*" you insisted.

I stood in the kitchen door and watched you fix supper. And you were so beautiful that I felt I had invented you— created you out of words in a poem—your hair rumpled and the gray wool slacks fitting you perfectly, and a heavy gold bracelet jangling from your wrist. "Who gave you the bracelet?" I asked.

You took some lettuce out of the refrigerator and began to wash it. "John."

"Your ex-husband?"

"Uh huh."

A tiny stab of pain went through me. "Why do you still wear it?"

"I dunno. It's pretty."

"I wish you wouldn't."

"Oh, Steven . . ."

"Please."

And so you removed the bracelet and dropped it in the drawer with the knives and forks. "Satisfied?"

"Yes. What was he like?"

You grinned. "Words fail me."

"Handsome?"

"God, no. And a dreadful prude."

"Like how?"

"I don't want to go into it, darling. It's a long story and I'll burn the dinner."

"Another time?"

You touched my hand. "Yes. Another time."

You set up a card table in front of the fire and we ate our steak there—the flowers I had brought you in a vase, and the bottle of wine unopened. You had dutifully applied a dab of the perfume, and scolded me for extravagance, and now we sat in silence, the meal over. Your face in the flickering light had an unreal quality, an aura of dream, and I could not stop gazing at it: the translucent skin and pale blond hair, the guarded blue eyes. Everything about you seemed fragile and strangely pure, and, without knowing why, I wanted to memorize you, to burn your image into my mind so that no matter what happened you would live inside me. I stared at your tapering hands, the smallness of your feet in their slippers—and a love as powerful as death swept through my heart. "Can we go to bed now?" I asked.

You walked over and kissed my forehead, and we went upstairs and undressed. The touch of you was keener than it had been the night before, more poignant, and yet everything was slow—drawn out like a ribbon of time. Everything was delicate, each of us exploring the other with new awareness, new gentleness, and I felt time expanding into the silence of the universe, felt the universe contract to the bed on which we lay, all existence focused on our hands and mouths. The rope of time—flung outward—came back again and wound about us. My mind became empty. I was a shell through which the ocean roared. I sank into fathoms where bells sounded. My mind vanished and a high-flung wave lifted me and carried me forward, mica and foam swirling about my eyes. I felt myself hurled into space, wreathed in seafoam, drowning and small in the torrent of the sea. I felt the crest of the wave carry me into the sky, curve against the arch of heaven, and crash back again to earth.

And then I slept.

twenty-three

I see a series of pictures now—snapshots—and they flash and click, each one real. I see us walking in the woods, our hands touching, stopping to watch a bird or a chipmunk. I see the woods turning slowly to warmth, revolving to sunlight, and I smell the dampness and the flowers. I see us stopping to kiss, Sam straining at his leash, the wind cold and yet touched with spring. I see us sitting on a stone bench, a cigarette between your fingers, your eyes a brilliant blue. Dampness and old leaves, ice melting, the springtime coming as tides come, a flood of light and flowers, and always the gray sky veering above our heads and a sound of tugboats. I see us standing in your kitchen, turning from a pile of unwashed dishes to embrace each other. I see myself coming up the stairs with wood for the fire.

I love you so terribly: the way you move through a room, no motion wasted, your body lithe and delicate. I love the way your thin hands hold a glass, an object, and the precision of these hands when they arrange a vase of flowers. I love the quick motion of your head as you turn to look at something—the flight of a bird against the evening sky—and the way you can break into laughter at the slightest provocation. I love the way you have tried to keep house for me, cooking diligent meals, changing the bed linens, and there are times when I pretend that we are married, alone for the rest of our lives, caught in a painted idyll where time will never hurt us, or change things, or destroy.

You are not the person I thought—all harshness vanished now that we are lovers. You are not the woman who opened the door that first day and stared at me, wild with loneliness and anger. You have stepped into the sunlight, and everything that touches you now touches me. What shall I give you, besides myself? What shall I buy? An old book of poems, a teacup, a single rose. What beautiful object can I give you—you who are already beautiful—what can I make? Poems and silence. Or find a bird's nest in a tree. Pick the first flowers of spring, gather small stones by the river. Hold everything roundly, as in a soap bubble: the Hudson, and sun glinting on the other shore, little trains weaving by and sudden sailboats buffeted by the wind. Let it all be held in a soap bubble, the world turned iridescent, green and gold. . . .

We lay in bed in the early twilight, our arms around each other, and I said, "What was he like, Hadley?"

"John?"

"Yes."

"Ah, darling . . ."

I kissed your shoulder. "Tell me."

"Why? It's so irrelevant."

"Not to me."

"Why do men always want to know about their rivals?"

"Is he a rival?"

"Of course not. It was years ago."

"Then what was he like?"

"I've told you. An aging Ph.D. candidate. An intellectual. A prude."

"Why did you marry him?"

"Because . . . oh, God, who knows? Because I was young and wild and wanted someone to restrain me. I don't know."

77

"Was he good in bed?"

"Darling, I've told you that bed is not a tennis match. People aren't good or bad at it."

"But we're good, aren't we?"

You stroked my face. "Yes. Yes."

"I love you so much, Hadley."

"I told you not to say that."

"Why?"

"Because it's always been bad luck for me. I'd rather think of us as passionate friends."

I laughed. "All right. Was he handsome—your husband?"

You sat up and reached for a cigarette on the night table. "He was neither handsome nor interesting nor nice. And, being a perverse human being, those are probably the reasons I married him."

"How did you meet?"

"I was living with a group of artists in Brooklyn Heights and John was a critic for one of the little magazines. He came to dinner one night, and decided to review my poems, and . . . oh, I don't know."

"Yes, you do. You just don't want to tell me."

"All right, all right. He came to dinner and I shocked him by using a few four-letter words, so he promptly asked me out."

"Why 'promptly'?"

"Because he was a born reformer, and I seemed to need reforming. I had had quite a few affairs, darling, and was

78

squandering my talent, and so he took me on as a project. His puritanism fascinated me. I mean, I had never known a man who wouldn't sleep with a woman before marriage. Also, he was terribly bright, in a Harvard sort of way, and came from a rich family."

"Did that matter to you?"

"Since I could barely pay my rent, yes. It did. We had intellectual dinners in candle-lit restaurants, and went to foreign films, and yet he would never make love to me. It got to be rather a game. So one night he drank too much wine and I seduced him—and he was so horrified that the next day he proposed."

"Did you like sleeping with him?"

"Oh, Steven . . ."

"Tell me."

"There's nothing to tell. He was a very repressed man, and in those days I thought of myself as a femme fatale. So I enjoyed educating him."

"Like me."

"No. *Not* like you."

I reached for your cigarette and took a drag on it. "I can't see you married, Hadley. It seems weird."

"It was. I couldn't keep house or anything. And I either burned his dinners or forgot to cook them at all. And whenever he brought friends home the place was a mess, and I had taken in three stray cats, and . . . no, that wasn't it. I'm telling it wrong."

"What was it then?"

"My work. My writing. After those wild oats were sown I got into work in a way that was pathological. I couldn't concentrate on him, or anyone. I only cared about my talent. Because . . . because if you're an artist, Steven, you don't own yourself. Your whole life is focused on the task you must do. And it isn't that you've chosen this task, or even wanted it. It's simply that it has been given you and you're stuck with it. It's the way saints are drawn to God—not because they want God, but because they cannot help the God that enters into them. Do you understand this?"

I took your hands and kissed them. "Yes. I think so."

"But the strange thing is that it robs you of love. So there you are—like me—unable to love your parents, cruel to your husband, and unwilling to have a child."

"He wanted one?"

"Oh, yes. Terribly. He wanted a son. And the idea of it frightened me so much that I left him—and then we were divorced."

"What you're saying is that a person can't have both life and art. Isn't that it?"

You pulled away from me. And in the dim light I could see a look of suffering in your eyes. "Yes, I guess so. But I don't think any of it was worth it. It's stopped me from giving."

But you're giving to me! I thought. You're giving me everything, and I don't even know why. There is a reason for it, but you'll never tell me until you're forced to, and maybe not even then. You are giving to me. . . .

twenty-four

It is so wild, so strange: our life upon this earth. The strength of our personalities, the impact of our deeds. Whole cities rise from the hands of men, and music is written, and poems, and people illuminate the darkness like great candles—their souls on fire with the energy of living. And their presence is such that you can feel them a thousand miles away. Their presence is such that you know they will endure forever, their single spark lighting the heavens. This one a poet, that one a mathematician. One able to make music, another capable of touching stars. So real, so tangible, so immutably alive.

And then snuffed out by the wind. A small flame quenched.

And silence.

twenty-five

I looked at you and there was light in your face—an emanation of dawn. And your pale hair was tangled and your eyes, for once, were not withheld from me. Your mouth, bruised from kissing, was soft, and the warmth of your arms around me sent a kind of pain through my heart. I prayed that it would last forever, that some unknown force would keep us this way always—locked into one another, body against body, mind into mind—and so deeply at peace after lovemaking that we would fall asleep at once, our bodies still entangled. Waking, I looked at you, and there was light in your face. Morning. Dawn.

"Hadley . . ."

"What, dearest?"

"Will it always be like this?"

"Us, you mean?"

"Yes."

"Yes—of course."

"Are you sure?"

"Why do you ask me, Steven?"

"I don't know. I get frightened."

You pulled my head down on your breast and drew the covers over us. "Silly. There's nothing to be afraid of. I take care of you, don't I?"

"Yes."

"And you take care of me. So everything's all right."

"I don't know. It's just that sometimes I don't understand why this has happened to me. Or if I deserve it or anything."

You stroked my hair. "There's no such thing as deserving. Everyone deserves everything."

"But you're so good to me."

"It's easy to be good to you."

"Why?"

"Because you're so unaware of yourself: your talent, your beauty."

"Men aren't beautiful."

You traced my mouth with your fingertips. "That, my darling, is where you're wrong."

"And compared to you, I have no talent."

"Comparisons are foolish."

"Hadley . . . do you really think I will be a poet?"

"I don't know, sweetheart. If it's meant to happen, it will happen. People don't have much to say about their lives."

"How do you mean?"

"Life happens to us. It's only an illusion that we impose ourselves on it. Don't you see? *It* happens to us—and the best we can do is to be open and receptive about it."

"I don't agree with that at all."

You smiled. "I see. Why not?"

"Because if there's no free will . . . then nothing makes any sense."

"I didn't say there wasn't free will."

"Oh."

"But if you were meant to be a poet, you will be one. That's all."

"I want it so much."

"I know."

"I would die for you, Hadley."

"I don't want to hear that."

"You never let me tell you things."

"Because they don't need to be told."

"But . . ."

"Shh. We don't need words any longer, do we?"

"No."

"Then touch me—and forget the words."

twenty-six

We are together—softly—and the room is rich with spring and darkness. In the forest a lone bird sings and night shrouds time with deepest velvet. We are together in this room, clinging to a piece of the universe, and I do not know where one of us ends and the other begins. We are together in the mind of the world, the mind of the God you believe in. Our roots go down into earth and grow entwined. We are together like plants, vines, merging rivers, together like drowning men in a depthless sea. Hadley, all the mountaintops are shining with the thin gold of dawn and all the deserts are streaked with purple pools, shadows. All the seas rise up, frozen and green, whipped with foam, because we are together. Because of all the people on earth, blind wanderers, we have found each other. We are together—and flights of swallows lace the trees with silver. On the black sea a path of coins is flung toward us, beckoning, asking us to dive more deeply. Seaweed tangles our hair, cathedral bells sound in the tide, the veering sky opens to an azure vault—soundlessly—and the blue and white marble of the world spins slowly so as not to spill its lakes and rivers. Endlessly. Soundlessly. And all because of one small and simple thing. We are together. Together in one bed.

twenty-seven

And then it crashed—everything falling, changing, splitting apart like pieces of a puzzle, my whole life disappearing before my eyes and I, frozen and uncomprehending, unable to act.

Even now, writing these words, something goes tight inside me. Even now, remembering my shock and bafflement, my sheer incredulity at the way you were gliding away from me, vanishing while I still held you, made love to you. . . . And it all happened so suddenly that summer that I did not understand it: your absence when I would arrive in the afternoons, and your growing evasions. Suddenly you had appointments. Suddenly you were driving to the next town, five miles away, only to return home pale and drawn, needing a drink. Suddenly you began to lose weight—markedly, dramatically—and the excuses for all this varied by the hour. One day you would tell me that you were going to "the library," and the next day it was "Dr. Marks." But what's wrong with you? I would ask. "Nothing, darling. Just some stupid kind of anemia. I'm taking vitamin shots." But you would return from these trips so exhausted that I would be frightened.

"Hadley—where have you been? I've been waiting an hour."

"The doctor. I told you yesterday."

"You didn't."

"All right, so I didn't."

You threw down your handbag and looked around the room. "What are you looking for?" I asked.

You smiled. "I don't know."

I touched your arm. "What's wrong with you, Hadley?"

"I *told* you. It's a form of anemia. Jesus, Steven, leave me alone."

"But you're acting so weird . . ."

"I'm not."

"You are."

"Stop harassing me!"

"I'm not harassing you—but you're different."

"I've been working too hard, that's all."

"I thought you said it was anemia."

"Oh God, here we go again . . ."

You sank down on the couch and I stood there like a stranger—not knowing if you were lying or telling the truth. Your linen skirt was wrinkled, and the silk blouse was drenched in sweat. You kicked off your sandals, leaned back and shut your eyes, and I was left alone. . . . I look back on these scenes and find them incredible, yet I must have been so ignorant of illness in those days that I misunderstood every symptom: the dramatic weight loss, the lack of appetite, your increasing irritability.

I began to cook your meals and do the housework. I began to treat you gingerly, like someone who could explode at the slightest provocation. And indeed, your anger was growing into something weird and irrational. One day you would scream at me that there was no food in the refrigerator—the next day you would complain that all the food in the refrigerator made you sick. You were paranoid about the supply of liquor—it was never enough, I must be drinking it or giving it away—and stopped paying your bills, so that the lights were turned off one day. You began to go through boxes of letters, looking for things that could never be found. You began to burn manuscripts. And when I complained that manuscripts were important, you looked at me and laughed.

One afternoon we lay down together to make love, and had a fight instead. I could not believe it, for you were transformed before my eyes, rising abruptly to put on your clothes before we had even begun.

"What's wrong?" I asked.

"Leave me alone, Steven. I mean it."

"But why won't you . . ."

"Because I'm tired, that's why! Tired of your hands all over me."

"Hadley . . ."

"What is it with you? Do you need sex every minute? Go home and stop pawing me. I'm sick of making love."

I stared at you and saw hatred in your face—and then I stumbled out of the house in shock, a feeling of imminent loss pervading me like nausea. And from that day on we fought, crazily, stupidly, you unwilling to make love, and the sudden deprivation of sex turning me violent and childish.

"But why can't we?"

"Because I'm tired of you."

"That's a lie. You love me."

"Love? Are you mad? A few rolls in the hay . . ."

I grabbed you roughly. "We love each other!"

"I never said I loved you. Go home and stop all this."

"I won't go home."

"Very well, then—I'll throw you out."

"Why have you changed? Why . . ."

"Why, why, why! Everything is *why* with you."

"You never tell me the truth!"

"So what! So the hell what!"

Each of these scenes occurred while you were high on pills or gin—so high that it was like reasoning with a mad-woman—and the pills increasing now to the point where I knew it was dangerous. I knew that you started to drink upon rising in the morning, that you no longer worked on your book, and that you were stumbling through life like a zombie. I knew that your trips to the doctor were increasing too, and yet, unbelievably, I did not connect the pills and gin with what you called your "anemia." Never once did it occur to me that pain as sharp as fire was searing you, dragging at your insides like stones, that you were being eaten alive by disease and no way to stop it. Nor

could I have known that you had refused cobalt, chemo-
therapy—all the treatments for cancer—so that if you had
to die, you would die like a human being and not an object.
You refused everything but drugs for pain, and yet you
clung to life in a way that was huge: going for walks in the
middle of the night, putting on records and dancing drunk-
enly about the living room, playing wild games with
Sam. . . .

My mind shifts like a kaleidoscope, and I see you throw-
ing Sam's rubber toys across the room—"Go get it, Sam!
Go!"—and then stumbling to the kitchen for a drink. I
see you refusing to open the front door for me, and finally
relenting. "Oh, Christ. All right, come in. But I will not go
to bed with you. Do you understand?" And so what had
been our lovemaking was now tossed away like a coin, and
what had been tenderness between us was now a joke.
"You know how to make out, Steven, so go get a girl. *Get
someone your own age.*" Because age had become, at last,
a topic between us, the most terrible of topics, and one that
you would not leave alone. "I'm old enough to be your
mother. Don't you know that? It's positively obscene."

I raged and wept and went home—only to return an
hour later, begging to be let in, demanding explanations.
But there were no explanations anymore, because to ex-
plain was to be sober and you were always drunk. . . . I did
not know what had hit me and began to go to pieces myself: skipping school, standing numbly in your driveway
when you would not unlock the door, writing you letters,

phoning you, and you not answering the phone. To taunt me, I thought. To hurt me.

Then the truth of it came. To get rid of me.

Because of course that was it. Everything you were doing was for the purpose of alienating me. Your withdrawal of sex, your cruel jokes at my manhood, your constant mention of age, age, age.

"You're such a baby, Steven. Such a bore. Can't you find a girl your own age?"

"You didn't use to care about my age."

"Well, I do now. You make me feel ridiculous."

"Why? Because I love you?"

"The only person you love, my friend, is yourself."

One day I realized in amazement that I was beginning to hate you—that at times I wished you dead. It was as if some terrible magician had waved a wand over us, distorting our features and filling our hearts with violence. I did not know if all this had happened in a matter of weeks or days, but a page had been turned, a chapter ended, and we would never be the same.

At last I left you, in a storm of grief and anger, convinced that your drug addiction had taken a turn for the worse and that because of it, you wanted none of me. And if I have any guilt, Hadley, it is this: that I abandoned you when you were most in need. I let you go out of pure ignorance, but it all seemed to make so much sense, because you had been on pills and liquor when I met you. Even then. And I shall never forget our last evening because it was one of the few times that summer that we were briefly happy—the sky washed with lavender and a scent of flowers in the room. You even kissed me in front of the open window, lingeringly with your tongue, and laughed as you felt my excitement.

"I still excite you, then?"

"Yes," I mumbled, my arms around you.

"And you still want me?"

"Yes."

"Why do you look like you're about to cry?"

I swallowed hard. "Because you've shut me out."

"Nonsense. It's just that . . . that this anemia thing has gotten worse and I don't feel like sex. That's all."

"Then why do you kiss me?"

You took my face in your hands. "Because you are beautiful. And young. All the things I'm not."

"You will always be beautiful, Hadley. Nothing will ever change that."

You smiled sadly. "You think so?"

"I know it."

"Enough. I'm tired. I want a drink. No . . . I just want to lie down. God. I feel like hell. Will you bring me a drink?"

You lay down on the sofa with Sam, and I brought you some gin and sat on the floor beside you. "I'm sorry I've been so awful lately," you said.

"It's OK."

"No, it isn't. But I can't seem to help it. Poor darling— you look like you've been through a war."

"It's OK," I said again.

"Shall I recite something? We haven't done much poetry lately."

"All right. One of yours?"

"No, no. A much better poet than me—Conrad Aiken."

"You don't often say that people are better than you."

"I know. But tonight I feel that everyone is better than me. Even Vincent Millay. But this poem . . . do you want to hear some of it?"

"Yes. Of course."

You reached for my hand and held it.

> *What is the flower? It is not a sigh of color,*
> *Suspiration of purple, sibilation of saffron,*
> *Nor aureate exhalation from the tomb.*
> *Yet it is these because you think of these,*
> *An emanation of emanations, fragile*
> *As light, or glisten, or gleam, or coruscation,*
> *Creature of brightness, and as brightness brief.*
> *What is the frost? It is not the sparkle of death,*
> *The flash of time's wing, seeds of eternity;*
> *Yet it is these because you think of these.*
> *And you, because you think of these, are both*
> *Frost and flower, the bright ambiguous syllable*
> *Of which the meaning is both no and yes.*

"Do you like that?" you asked.

"Yes," I said.

Suddenly we were kissing again—gently—my hands

stroking your face and breasts, and my mind spinning us into that bed upstairs where we had known so much love. And I knew that no matter what happened, I would worship you always for this: this miracle of closeness, and warmth, and desire.

You pulled away, and your eyes were like coals in your face. "I told you to leave me alone."

"But . . ."

"I told you!"

"Then why do you tease me? Make me want . . ."

"You, you! Always you! Can't you stop thinking of yourself? Why should it always be you?"

"You shouldn't tease me!"

"Nor should there be war or famine, my dear boy. But there are."

"It isn't fair."

"Dear God, are we talking about *fairness?*"

"Please come upstairs."

You threw back your head in rage. "In the name of Christ, go away! Can't you get the picture, Steven? *This relationship is over.* I am tired. And I am not feeling well. And all you are is a selfish little brat who thinks of nothing but getting laid."

I rose to my feet. "You bitch. I hate you."

"Good!"

"I mean it—I despise you."

"Then get the hell out of here and don't come back!"

"All right!" I shouted. "If that's what you want!"

"Get out of this room!"

"You filthy bitch!"

You jumped to your feet and slapped me, hard across the mouth, and it was over—both of us stunned by our anger, and a wall risen between us like stone.

twenty-eight

I remember, before our parting, how the spring came: a dazzle of blossoms against a world so pure that one could drown in it. I remember the rain-soaked woods and the delicate willows, green against a slate sky. But always I remember the blossoms, white and pink, intricate like lace, their fragrance making me vague and causing me to wander aimlessly, my mirrored eyes reflecting the sudden glint of airplanes. I had never known that the skies of spring were gray and that against them all life came violently, color spilling upon color like rainbows swirled in a glass. And the spring came so quickly, so fully, that I hardly noticed one day that it was summer and that the sky now burned with orange, dense heat and river haze.

School ended, my freshman year was over, and with it my life, all meaning gone after our parting. And what is so incredible is that nobody knew. I sat at the family dinner table, said words and heard words, went to the store for groceries, repaired an old car with my father—yet none of them saw that my soul had gone out like a candle and that the life in me was quenched.

How is it possible to live this way? To be swept with thoughts of suicide and mutilation—a longing for death as sweet and strong as sex—and nobody knowing, nobody seeing at all. How is it possible to be born out of the very blood of one's parents, their bone and flesh, and be unknown to them? To this day my mother turns the pages of photograph albums, thinking that the pictures show a family, and unaware that the eyes who gaze from those snapshots are the eyes of ghosts. Two grownups and two children: standing in the midst of their holidays like strangers in a strange land. Easter and Christmas. New clothes. Sally holding a kitten. And our frame house —wreathed in the death of dreams.

On the surface they asked me questions. Why was I so quiet, so absentminded? They suggested projects for the summer and wondered why I wasn't seeing Jerry or hanging around the community swimming pool. My mother complained that I never got any fresh air, and my father suggested that I work in his store for a few weeks at a good salary. . . . But this is not relevant, not relevant at all. Because the only human being I loved on earth was gone.

One night in August when I finally believed that I would never see you again—that our relationship was over —I walked down to the Hudson, took off my clothes and swam out into the dense green murk. Swam out far enough to know that I would not get back—but then turned and made it back, dragging myself through mud and reeds to collapse on the littered sandy shore. And that was how I learned I had no courage, not even the twisted courage of suicide, and so I spent the rest of the night lying there, imagining New York City fifty miles away: its skyline a crush of jewels against the smoky heavens, the George Washington bridge looping the Hudson like a spiderweb, and traffic on the West Side highway threading its way towards a majestic sprawl of haze and color and light. I knew you had returned there, but had not even sent you a note or looked up your phone number.

For your house was closed now—nailed shut like a ghost mansion and the weeds grown high—all sign of you vanished and drowned, swept away as though you had never existed. And sometimes I would go down there in the night to stare at the blank windows and say your name aloud, dreaming that the sound of you would bring you back, saying "Hadley" over and over like a chant. Because once you had told me about mystics who prayed perpetually, until they no longer said the prayer but the prayer said them, and so I made my prayer of you and tried to say you into the very marrow of my blood. As if the words would bring you home and stop all time in its wandering. As if the words could change the universe and turn the seasons back to snow.

It seemed like generations had passed since we had known each other. It seemed like yesterday. It seemed as though I had grown old while you remained unchanged, fixed and static like a figure on a vase, your beauty held and quivering. And sometimes, lying in the tall grass by the vacant house, it really seemed as though I touched you and tasted your mouth on mine—hallucinations swarming me like butterflies, memories and images webbing me with dream. I saw those days when we had spun with silver and the blossoms over our heads had brought the spring with clearest music. I stroked the soft tall grasses and said my prayer—your name—and prayed to die.

twenty-nine

Pain turned me inward and I became unreal. I moved in a haze of blue light. In the summer heat I was cold—and talking to people I seemed not to talk. Pain turned me inward, sensation gone. I felt numb, frozen, splintered like glass. I felt that I had unwound myself like a cord. My mind was a sea, tossed with memories, and these memories were the weight of statues pulling me under. Amid the swaying yellow grasses I saw your eyes. Bells chimed eerily and I heard you whisper, "Touch me, Steven. Ah, darling . . ." Voices echoed, rising and falling as ships rise, and I saw light slanting through the sea, heard cathedral bells sound in the tide. A swaying greenness, a trembling net of green and gold. "Touch me, Steven," and the bells sounding. "Touch me, Steven," and the months falling and spinning and dancing away from me like foam.

thirty

One night, early in September, the lights were on in your house and a car was parked in the driveway. Standing in the woods I felt my heart clench like a fist, and a hundred images raced through my mind. A moment later I threw open the front door and ran wildly up the stairs, calling your name.

But the person who turned to greet me was a man—thin, with gray hair, who was packing books into a cardboard box. I saw him and came to a halt in the doorway.

"Yes?" he said. "Can I help you?"

I could not speak for staring at the room and its desolation: sheets covering the furniture and cold gray ashes piled in the fireplace. The air was musty and dank and the card table you had always worked at, by the window, was gone.

"Yes?" the man said again.

"I. . . I was looking for Hadley. Mrs. Norman, I mean."

The man gazed at me. "She moved out in July."

"I know."

He straightened up and I saw that he was wearing an immaculate tan suit and a conservative tie. His shoes were dark and well-polished.

"Perhaps I can help you," he said.

"I don't know. I . . ."

"Are you a neighbor?"

"Yes. My name is Steven Harper."

"Mine is John Norman."

I felt nothing when I realized who he was, absolutely nothing, because it all seemed to have happened before—like a film one has seen many times on television. "You're a friend of Hadley's?" he asked.

"Yes. In a way. We used to work together."

"In what sense?"

"Poetry."

"Oh. You mean you studied with her."

"Yes."

"How odd. I wasn't aware that she had been teaching."

"We were friends," I said.

The man arched one eyebrow and smiled. And in that smile was a world that I instantly despised: a universe of snobbery and tightness and contempt. A world of contemplating other people from a great distance. Especially the young.

"I was her lover," I said.

The smile disappeared from his face. "What did you say?"

I sat down by the fireplace—slowly, deliberately. "I said that I was her lover. We broke up in June."

The man's face was white. "You must be joking."

"No. I'm not."

He sat down opposite me—wearily—as though he had

been through many trials in the last few days and had not expected another.

"Hadley and I. . . were married at one time."

"I know. She told me about you."

"I see. And when did you last speak to her?"

"I told you. In June."

Why do you hate him? I asked myself. You've only just met him and you hate him like death. You hate him so much that you could kill him. That neat, lightweight, expensive suit. Those polished shoes.

John Norman's eyes took me in more fully, and I saw that disbelief was still flooding him: amazement that someone my age had slept with his wife. "You're not pulling my leg about this?" he asked.

"Definitely not."

"I see. Well. Have you been in touch with Hadley?"

"No. We had a disagreement."

"And you haven't talked on the phone?"

I couldn't understand why he was asking me the same question over and over, and the longer I sat in the room with him, the more my hatred of him grew. I saw that he was devious and secretive—that he would never say anything straight out—and I realized how dreadful such people were. People whose minds were churning endlessly but who never told you the truth.

"Why do you keep asking me if I've talked to her?" I said.

"No reason, really."

"Is Hadley all right?" I asked suddenly. "She was sick last spring."

"How do you mean—sick?"

"I don't know. Some sort of anemia. She was losing weight."

"And drinking too much, I suppose?"

"Yes. Is she all right?"

"How long did you know her?" he asked.

"Around seven months."

"And you're not pulling my leg about . . ."

I looked him straight in the eye. "Why do you find it so weird? That we were lovers, I mean."

"I'm not entirely sure. It's just that I know Hadley rather well and . . ."

"You don't know her at all," I replied. And even as I said the words I realized that I had never behaved this way before. With complete confidence. Not caring what the outcome would be.

I glanced at the cardboard box. "Why are you packing her things?"

"No reason, really. She asked me to help her out."

"But how come she didn't take them with her?"

"I'm not really sure."

And then I knew that something was wrong—terribly wrong—because this man was lying to me in a way that made no sense.

"She's ill," I said.

John Norman was avoiding my eyes, contemplating the

cold ashes in the fireplace. "Well, yes. She's been in and out of the hospital."

I rose abruptly to my feet. "And she's in the hospital now?"

"Well . . . yes."

I grabbed his arm. "What's wrong with her?"

He brushed me off with distaste, as though I were an insect.

"Now look here . . ."

"Tell me!"

"My dear boy . . ."

"I'm not your dear boy! And I've got to know what's wrong with her. We love each other."

He flashed me a look of rage. "I find that hard to believe."

"Well, *I* find it hard to believe that you were married to her. But what difference does it make?"

John Norman lit a cigarette and stared at the match for a moment. "She has cancer," he said.

I sank down on the couch. "Since . . . when?"

"I don't know. For about a year, I suppose. Nobody knew."

I could not trust myself to speak and so I simply gazed at him.

"I'm sorry you are forcing me to discuss this," he said, "because as far as I am concerned, it's Hadley's business and no one else's. Hadley is a very private person. But if the two of you were . . . intimate, as you say, then perhaps you have a right. I don't know. To be perfectly frank with you, the entire situation astounds me."

"What situation?"

"Your affair with her."

"How long has she been in the hospital?"

"Since August."

"And why was she living out here?" I asked.

"Everyone thought she was in Europe—even her agent. The only way I found out about this was because we share the same doctor and he finally told me. Against her wishes, I might add."

"But why was she . . ."

"Oh, how do I know?" he said angrily. "She wanted to go through the illness alone, I suppose, without people fussing over her. Hadley has always been very stubborn, very recalcitrant. She destroyed all her papers, you know, and they were priceless. Letters, manuscripts . . . ah well, what's the use?"

It was you she was getting away from, I thought. And now I see why. Because whether you're divorced or not you have never left her alone, and if you'd learned about her illness you would have driven her crazy. Harassed her and harassed her. Given her no peace. She came out here because she wanted privacy—and privacy is something you make a big thing about but don't even understand.

"Have you been to the hospital?" I asked him.

He looked at me coldly. "Of course. I've gotten her the best specialists in New York."

"And what do they say?"

For a moment the silence between us was visible: a thing of colors and shadows and light. "They say she's going to die," he answered.

"I don't believe you."

John Norman crushed his cigarette out in the ashtray. "Look—let's not prolong this any longer than we need to. I'm tired and irritable, and as far as I am concerned, you are just one more complication in the whole business. She has about three weeks to live."

I rose to my feet. "What hospital?"

"I don't want you to bother her. She's been through enough."

"I asked you what hospital!"

A strange look passed over his face. "Very well. Columbia-Presbyterian. But I'd rather you didn't . . ."

"Oh, go to hell," I said tiredly. "You stupid man. Just go to hell."

thirty-one

I sat in the bus and the world sped past me. Steel-gray water, black clouds, thundery sky. A sprawling panorama of factories and river towns. A gray canvas of diners, used car lots, Dairy Queen stands. Gazing into the storm-tossed air I saw barges moving along the Hudson loaded with gypsum, saw the sudden white wing of a sailboat, saw a tiny seaplane skim the water like a dragonfly. All of it swam together, merging and blurring like a dream.

You, who said you never gave to people, had given me the last months of your life.

Had taken me into your solitude.

Had offered me love.

My youth for your age. My songs for your dying.

These thoughts were so terrible that I struck my fist against the bus window, feeling pain ripple my hand and wanting more pain. I understood everything now, all the threads coming together and everything making sense: our meeting, our love, and our violent separation. You had pushed me out of your world to protect me, and in the midst of my grief I felt rage, wondering why older people always tried to protect the young.

I could not believe my own stupidity. Could not believe that I had watched you struggle through weeks of pain, challenging death like an adversary, then ignoring it, plunging into life like a swimmer holding the sea in his arms. I remembered you walking in the woods, touching things with the wonder of a child, stopping suddenly to gaze up at the tangled blossoms of spring.

To cease to exist. Breath gone. And taste. And desire.

Let me go through it with her, I prayed to the God I did not believe in, and if death is dreadful, then let me know the full dreadfulness of it. And if she is afraid, let me hold her. And if there is pain, let me feel it too. She is my reason for being and she has entered me like sun—a diamond light slanting into my eyes, making sharp what was blurred and catching facets of the rainbow. I have swum in this light, both myself and her, and something beyond us both. She is my reason for existence, and I have loved her so much that a part of me has become her: a person dreaming for years and then waking in a shower of gold, leaves tumbling like coins and a woman walking down a country road. I felt that I was real for the very first time—sleep drifting from my eyes, my childhood over—and the ignorance I had clung to so passionately falling away like a garment.

Let me take the journey with her, no matter how far into darkness. Let my soul stay with hers until the last second of breath. Let us turn together in the same direction, and let me see what she sees: the raven and the sun.

thirty-two

The hospital corridor was painted a pale shade of green, and the chairs in the lounge were green—making me feel that I was submerged in water, unable to move. Yet my feet carried me along the polished linoleum with a life of their own and my eyes glanced into various rooms. I saw a child standing by the bed of an old man. I saw a family clustered around the bed of a teenage girl. Plants, TV sets, trays of food. . . I realized that I was saying the room numbers aloud. 309, 311, 313. And finally your room—315—the door closed and the corridor suddenly empty, no one to be seen, no sound, no life.

I stood there for a long time, my mind a blank, and then I knocked and went in.

The first thing I noticed was that the room was large and bright: vases of flowers and a pile of books on the windowsill. I saw a new television set in the corner and a blue robe draped over a chair. I looked at you.

The shock was so great, Hadley, so unexpected, that my eyes left your face almost at once and I found myself trembling. Images stumbled through my mind. A child's paper-doll, flowers pressed in a book, dry leaves. You had grown so thin . . . so small.

"Hello," you said, not looking at me. "Come in."

"OK," I said. "Thanks."

Your right hand was smoothing the blanket with great care, and it was a full minute before I noticed your left hand—a needle strapped into its vein, and a plastic tube running from the needle to a bottle overhead.

"John told me you were coming," you said.

"Oh. He told you."

"Yes."

"Is this a bad time?"

"No. Not really."

I saw that you could not bring your eyes to meet mine. And now, gazing at you at last, I saw the incredible change in you: the emaciated arms and smoothly brushed hair. The ravaged face. All vitality had been drained away, all movement and color and light.

I crossed to the window and gazed at the river. The flowers in the vase had a sickly smell, as though they had been there for a long time. "You've got a good view," I said.

"Uh huh."

"And the . . . the hospital seems very nice."

"It is."

There was a pause while I stood at the window, and finally you said, "I'm sorry I look so awful. It must be a shock."

"No. Honest. You look fine."

"What a bad liar you are, Steven. You're white as a sheet."

"Oh."

"Did you come by bus?"

"Yes."

The door opened and a nurse came in with a plant wrapped in gold paper. Smiling, she placed it on the bureau and left the room. "Do you want to see the card?" I asked.

"No."

You leaned back on the pillow and I realized how tired you were—how exhausting it was for you to speak—and my throat went tight at the pallor of your skin and the dreadfulness of that needle strapped to your hand. A small blue vein stood out on your forehead, and your lips were parched and dry.

"Don't talk if it tires you," I said.

"It's all right. But I don't want a lot of recriminations. You know?"

"Sure."

"I mean, I don't want to go over the whole thing."

"I know. I won't."

"Thank you."

You could have been a stranger, Hadley—some unknown person lying in a hospital bed—and I could not find the thing that was keeping us so far apart. I wanted to go over to you and touch you, take your hand, but these gestures were impossible. I was rooted where I stood, and because I did not know what else to do I stared at the objects on the night table: a box of Kleenex, a paper cup, a white comb. All of them seemed to belong to someone else, some woman who bore your name and face, but who was an impostor.

"Is Sam OK?" I asked after a while.

"Yes. He's with John."

"John Norman?"

"Uh huh."

"But . . ."

"It's all right. John's kind to animals."

You closed your eyes and moistened your lips with your tongue. "Have you been writing?"

"No," I said. "Not lately."

"Try to get back to it soon."

"OK."

"Promise?"

"Yes. Sure."

"Hadley," I said awkwardly, "are . . . you in pain?"

"No—they're giving me morphine."

"Oh. I see."

There was nothing left to say. And I could not believe it, because I had had so much to say coming down on the bus, thousands of words crowding my mind, words hoarded for months, a treasure-house of words, and now not one of them suitable. You were as far away from me as you had ever been—the unknown thing keeping us on opposite sides of a wall—and for the very first time I felt the difference in our ages, felt inadequate and helpless and young.

"I'm sorry I'm not more talkative," you murmured.

"That's all right. Just rest."

"I thought I would be feeling stronger today, but I had a bad night. You understand?"

"Yes. It's OK."

"I'm sorry."

"It doesn't matter."

And then, without thought or knowledge, I knew that the thing between us—the unknown thing—was death, and that we would never be close again. I knew that you had begun to make a journey and thus had separated yourself from me, taking your things over one by one: your poems and your memories, and all the places you had ever lived, and the people you had loved, and your childhood. You were carrying them gently to a place I couldn't see or share, and your preoccupation with this change was the thing that made you seem so far away. I knew that you were willing to leave now and that nothing on this earth concerned you anymore. Your words to me were mere politeness. A formality.

After a few moments you said, "Steven, would you mind going? I'm a bit tired."

"All right. If you want me to."

"I do, darling, and . . . and I want to ask something of you that's hard."

I came closer to the bed, my heart pounding. "Anything, Hadley. You know that."

"I want to ask you not to come here again."

"But . . ."

"It would help me if you didn't."

I felt the tears rise in my throat. "OK. If that's what you want."

"It is, sweetheart. And one other thing . . ."

"Yes?"

"Go back to your work."

"All right."

"And no regrets. OK?"

"OK," I said, walking to the door. But I could not say good-bye and so I simply stood there, my back to you and the tears flooding my throat.

"Steven?"

"Yes?"

"I loved you very much."

Because I could not speak, I nodded my head twice in your direction, and stood there for a moment longer, and then walked through the door . . . through the door and down the longest corridor of my life, the linoleum glinting and shining and sparkling like purest marble.

thirty-three

It is strange how little I felt during the next few weeks, how quiet I was inside—while outside me life began again with a surge. My sophomore year, and books to be bought and classes signed up for, and the familiar bus carrying me to the Community College each day. A new English teacher on the scene who was young for a change, and bright, and Jerry and I cautiously renewing our friendship, which had stopped almost a year ago.

Strange how empty I was. But I had suffered so much when we parted in June that there was little suffering left in me—only the image, from time to time, of your hand resting on the hospital bed, a needle in its vein. I would wake in the middle of the night with that hand before me and find my body bathed in sweat, my ears ringing, and would push myself back into sleep like someone seeking the depths of a pool. That hand . . . so thin, so vulnerable to the hurt that the needle must have caused. Your hand . . . changed and ravaged and scarred.

There were moments when your poetry would enter my

mind, the music echoing between mountains, my memory of each poem perfect and no way to blot out the words or ever forget them.

The clustering bees will outlive us, and even the gnats. And the hummingbird pierces the air with no cry, caught in its amber. Some things live forever, blinded by stars, and feed on the light.

One night I woke from a dream with the realization that there had been more between you and John Norman than you had told me—that indeed, you had been sleeping with him long after the divorce. I saw him packing your books into the cardboard box and heard you telling me that you had given Sam to him, Sam whom you loved better than anyone on earth. Other clues flashed into my mind: his gold bracelet on your wrist, his monogrammed shirts still among your clothes, and a novel I had found in the kitchen once whose inscription read: "To Hadley, who I can neither live with nor without. John."

So there were things I had not known—hundreds of them, perhaps—your past separating us like a desert. The best years of your life had been spent with people I had never seen, and your character had been molded by forces I would never understand. Suddenly I was bereft of everything—your childhood and the real reason you had been estranged from your parents. Your life in New York as a celebrity. Parties, friends, trips to Greece. And a woman named Ann Lowry who had loved you and painted your portrait. All the names, so casually dropped, of people who had shaped and shattered your life. And, most painfully, the men you had had: those nameless figures who had wakened at dawn and turned to you as the earth turns toward sunlight, holding you close as I had once held you, knowing that I would die if you did not love me, if your mouth did not touch mine. . . .

I wondered if you had ever belonged to me. I wondered if I had held you at all.

One Sunday morning, exactly four weeks after I had been to the hospital, a bulletin came over the radio that Hadley Norman, the prize winning American poet, had just died in New York City after a long illness. I listened to the announcement, felt strangely numb, and went to take a shower. The water was steaming hot, its needles striking my back with force, and I soaped myself for a long time and washed my hair. Then I dried myself with a new towel, dressed in a shirt and Levi's, and walked out into a day as fresh and clean as the first day on earth.

thirty-four

The story has no ending, Hadley. You died before your work was finished. I lived, and began my own. As though you had slipped a key in my pocket. As though you had handed me a torch and stepped away. Perhaps we each have a turn and you had given me mine—or perhaps you had relinquished your turn so that I might begin sooner, might seize the day while I was young. . . . I do not know, because the story does not end.

As long as I live, my heart will jump when I see a woman on the street who resembles you. For the rest of my life, I will walk into rooms and seek your face. And no matter who I touch or sleep with, there will always be an echo of another time—a moment when two people loved each other and the world was still. But one thing is certain: the transcendence of words. I dream these words and write them, and you appear again—perfect, immutable, caught in sunlight, alive with spring and the smell of flowers— and for one moment it is enough. For one small moment, placed in time, I know that to be a writer is to conquer grief, the petty strokes of fate, and the worst that man can do to man. For here upon this page you live.

And here—I begin.

About the Author

BARBARA WERSBA has published ten books for young people, among them *The Dream Watcher* and *Run Softly, Go Fast*. Miss Wersba also lectures on the subject of writing, has served as a judge for the National Book Awards, and reviews books for *The New York Times*. She lives in Rockland County, New York—in an old building that was once a country store—and does much of her work on the island of Martha's Vineyard.